THE QUILLER
MEMORANDUM

ADAM HALL

THE QUILLER MEMORANDUM

A TOM DOHERTY ASSOCIATES BOOK

NEW YORK

THE QUILLER MEMORANDUM

Copyright © 1965 by Jonquil Trevor

Introduction copyright © 2004 by Otto Penzler

Originally published by Simon and Schuster, Inc., in 1965.

A Forge Book
Published by Tom Doherty Associates, LLC
175 Fifth Avenue
New York, NY 10010

www.tor.com

Forge® is a registered trademark of Tom Doherty Associates, LLC.

Library of Congress Cataloging-in-Publication Data

Hall, Adam.
    The Quiller memorandum / Adam Hall.—1st Forge ed.
        p. cm.
    "A Tom Doherty Associates book."
    ISBN 0-765-30967-X   EAN 978-0765-30967-9 (hc acid-free paper)—ISBN 0-765-30968-8   EAN 978-0765-30968-6 (pbk. : acid-free paper)
    1. Quiller (Fictitious character)—Fiction. 2. Intelligence officers—Fiction. 3. British—Germany—Fiction. 4. Berlin (Germany)—Fiction. 5. Nazis—Fiction.
    I. Title.

PR6039.R518Q5 2004
823'.914—dc22

                                              2003069455

Printed in the United States of America

INTRODUCTION

The names of only a handful of espionage agents resonate with readers. While detectives are recognizable by the score—Holmes, Queen, Poirot, Wimsey, Spenser, Hammer, Marlowe, Spade, Archer, and on and on—a mere handful of spies are chosen for the pantheon of literary icons: James Bond, George Smiley, Matt Helm, Harry Palmer (nameless in Len Deighton's novels but given a name for the movies), Ashenden (based on his single eponymous book), maybe Modesty Blaise, and, of course, the pseudonymous Quiller.

There is a wide range of realism in the novels of these characters, from the nearly campy adventures of Bond and his female counterpart, Blaise, to the quiet ordinariness of Smiley, whose work is often rescued from tedium by the brilliant prose of his creator, John le Carré.

Quiller would not even agree that he is an espionage agent, noting that, if an assignment involved international espionage, M.I.5. or D.I.6. would step in and do the job it is expected to do. Quiller doesn't work for M.I.5 or D.I.6., hence he cannot be involved in espionage.

The agency for which he does work has no name. It does not, in fact, officially exist because it is expected to do things that the government could not publicly allow. Its top executives are unknown to the operatives, and their existence would be denied by the

British government. It is given assignments only from the level of the prime minister, and generally when the other branches of the law-enforcement community have turned down the assignment because it is too sensitive—or too dangerous.

Quiller is an operative who has been given a code name, just as all members of this secret bureau have been. That name is unknown to everyone except the highest level of executives at the agency.

An operative as elusive as Quiller is difficult to describe, and very difficult to understand. He is portrayed only obliquely in the books about him, but his creator wrote a biographical sketch of him about a quarter of a century ago, when Quiller was at the height of his fame. It appeared in a book titled *The Great Detectives*, which I edited and which was published by Little Brown (1978); it is somewhat abridged below:

> About his past there are various rumors: that he was someone in the professional category of lawyer or doctor, denied his license; that he once served a prison term, undeservedly (hence his bitterness, which is never far below the skin); that he is a man on the run who has found a perfect cover in the Bureau.
>
> In his forties, he is as fit as an alley cat and his whole makeup is tense, edgy, and bitten-cared. He needs to live close to the crunch. Like bullfighters and racing drivers, he is a professional neurotic, half in love with death.
>
> Obviously antisocial, shy of people and human contact, he is wary of giving anything of himself to others. But, on rare occasions when the pressures of a mission have forced him into a position where he must consider other people—sometimes a deadly opponent—he reveals compassion, surprising himself.
>
> His last will and testament is revealing: "Nothing of value, no dependents, next of kin unknown." This nihilistic aspect of his character, his isolationism, suits perfectly the atmosphere of the Bureau, where anonymity and facelessness are virtues. If all the requirements of the Bureau were put through a com-

puter to synthesize the ideal executive, they would result in Quiller.

Quiller has completed numerous missions—a tribute to his professionalism in a trade where life is cheap. He doesn't drink because it would affect his reaction time, and for the same reason he doesn't smoke. He refuses to carry a gun. Ever. He puts his reasons this way: "If a man has to carry a gun it means he's got no better resources. A gun can be more dangerous to you than to the other man, if you carry one. It gives you a false feeling of power, superiority, and you get the fatal idea that, with this thing in your hand, you don't have to make any effort because the conflict's already been won. And for Christ's sake watch it if you find you've left the safety catch on or forgot to load or there's a dud in the clip or the other man gets time to kick the thing out of your hand—then you've really had it. Better to use your brain because your brain won't stop working for you till you're dead. Guns are for amateurs, and anyway . . . I don't like the bang they make."

Quiller is often introspective, and likely to conclude that "You don't do what you do for the sake of your country or world peace, though you kid yourself. You do it to scratch an itch. I'm not talking about the people who do it for the money—they're just whores. Most of us do it because we don't get a big enough kick out of pushing a pen or punching the clock or washing the car on Sundays. We want to get outside of all that and live on our own so we can work off our scabby neuroses without getting arrested for it. We want to scratch the itch till it bleeds."

Quiller and four other executives at the Bureau have the suffix 9 appended to their code names. It means they've proved themselves reliable under torture. It's not an award of any kind, but an indication to directors that a man with the 9 suffix is suitable for sending into an area where "implemented interrogation" will be made if he is captured. Quiller's reaction to this ability to stand torture is straightforward. "Within a couple of hours," he says, "an efficient interrogator and his team can turn any man into a raving animal if they use the full technique. But they can't; there's a breakoff point because the whole idea is that they want information out of you and they know they won't get it if they've gone too far and wrecked the psyche. What you've got to do is try not to talk on this side of consciousness, because once you've flaked out you're safe till they start again. And if you can do it once, you can do it a dozen times."

His attitude toward women stems from his fear of people, his need to feel cut off and isolated. He chooses women who are themselves solitary, reserved, each in her own way a lone wolverine with some hurt to heal, a past to forget, or a lie to live. Some of them are seeking their own identity, as Quiller himself may be, and he finds himself attracted to them as reflections of his own enigma. They are lean and have quietness, are watchful, talking little, turning their heads slowly to appraise a newcomer, withdrawing with the speed of a spring if their approach is too immediate.

Quiller is versed in psychology, sleep dynamics, the nervous system and its behavior under stress. His fast-driving technique is based squarely on a knowledge of what happens to a car when it's pushed to the limit. He is aware of the target-finding values of positive and negative feedback as he makes his way through a mission. He is good enough at code-breaking—sometimes he is able to intercept a signal from an opposition cell without having to ask London.

Knowing Quiller to be difficult, obstinate, obdurate, and perverse, the directors at the Bureau handle him in the most appropriate way. They seldom offer him a mission outright, because it would give him the chance of refusing it out of sheer bloody-mindedness. They lead him into it with a carrot, working up his interest indirectly. "I understand," they'll say, for example, "they've landed Smythe with a real stinker, and frankly I don't think he can handle it." Or they'll just tell him this one "isn't for him" without saying why, so that he feels deprived of an important mission.

An executive can refuse to accept a mission for any one of a dozen reasons, but if he accepts it, he's totally committed, even to the point of using a cyanide capsule.

Quiller prefers working alone, on solo missions, accepting a director in the field where necessary but never working alongside other executives.

Once he has left his base and begins work in the field, he is usually at risk. If he is captured and interrogated, or if he is exposed to the opposition's view (perhaps holed up in a building or on a ship and unable to leave), or if there is the slightest risk of his giving away his base and his director in the field, he will cut himself loose and take the consequences—just as any other executive would. If he is slow to do this, the director will do it for him.

Quiller once had to brief a recruited agent: "You've got to learn to cross the line and live your life outside society, shut yourself away from people, cut yourself off. Values are different out there. Let a man show friendship for you and you've got to deny him, mistrust him, suspect him, and nine times out of ten you'll be wrong but it's the tenth time that'll save you from a dirty death in a cheap hotel because you'd opened the door to a man you thought was a friend. Out there you'll be alone and you'll have no one you can trust, not even the people who are running you. Not even me. If you make the wrong kind of mistake at the wrong time in the wrong place, and it looks like you're fouling up the mission or exposing the Bureau, they'll throw you to the dogs. And so will I."

This situation is accepted by the executives. So is the fact that they are expendable if the crunch comes or a wheel falls off. The executive is cut loose the instant he presents a risk to the network, to the Bureau. The working phrase is: "The mission is more important than the man."

Quiller made his debut in *The Quiller Memorandum* (published in the U.K. as *The Berlin Memorandum)* in 1965 and won the Edgar Award for Best Novel in 1966. This nail-biting thriller about a large number of Nazis who escaped retribution after World War II and, using new identities, rose to power in West Germany in the hopes of creating a new Reich, was immediately made into a very successful film starring George Segal, with a screenplay by Harold Pinter, in 1966. In 1975, Quiller served as the basis for a British television series.

Although *The Quiller Memorandum* was the first of nineteen books to feature the virtually indestructible agent, the author had written many earlier novels under his own name, Elleston Trevor. This remarkable man, a former RAF pilot who began writing after his WWII service, died only a few years ago. He had written more than fifty books using several pseudonyms, aside from Adam Hall, Mansell Black, Simon Rattray, and Caesar Smith. The best known of these novels, perhaps, is *The Flight of the Phoenix*, which memorably starred James Stewart, in the movie version.

The Quiller series managed that rare combination of popular success, with millions of copies sold worldwide, and critical acclaim. *Harper's* magazine called that first book, *The Quiller Memorandum*, "brilliant . . . one of the best spy novels ever," and it received (in addition to the Edgar) the French Grand Prix de Littérature Policière. The last book in the series, *Quiller Balalaika*, was recently published, but the other excellent novels in this important series are currently out of print. They will be back. Take my word for it. Like Quiller himself, these books will live on and on.

—OTTO PENZLER
New York

THE QUILLER
MEMORANDUM

1 | POL

A couple of air-hostesses came in through the glass doors, crisp and pure-looking in Lufthansa uniform. They looked once at the group of pilots who stood at the soft-drinks bar and then swung on their spiked heels to preen themselves in the mirrors. The pilots turned to watch them, all of them tall, all of them blond. Nobody spoke. Another girl came in and touched her reflected hair before she turned away and studied her shining fingertips at arm's length, glancing up just once at the tall blond men, looking down again with her head tilted, admiring her spread fingers as if they were flowers.

One of the young men grinned and looked among his friends to see who would join him in an approach toward the girls, but nobody moved. A light flashed rhythmically across and across the window, coming from the airport beacon. The two girls left the mirrors, glanced again at the pilots, and then stood neatly with their feet together and their hands behind them. Everybody seemed to be waiting.

The boy who had grinned to his friends seemed to venture a step toward the hostesses, but another blocked his foot and the boy shrugged, folding his arms. Into the silence was rising the sound of a jet airliner starting up outside. This was what they had been waiting for and they all turned toward the center, looking upward, listening, all of them smiling now.

The rising sound of the aircraft was not yet very loud, so that I heard the door of the box being opened behind my chair; a wedge of light came against the wall and then went out.

Clearly visible through the big window the dorsal lamp of the airliner began winking, and the sound of the jets leveled out to an even pitch. The pilots tensed and the hostesses took a few delicate eager steps toward the doors, with their bodies turned to face the group of boys.

I was aware that someone had come into the box and was standing behind me. I did not turn my head.

Then the pilots moved in a body toward the center, and the prettiest of the girls flung out her hands and called eagerly: *"Who's for the air?"*

The tallest of the boys responded: *"I am!"* His friends chorused to the first notes of the music: *"We are!"*

"Who's for the sky?" sang the girls, and they were into the number.

Under cover of the music, the man sat down in the chair next to mine, shifting it at an angle so that he could face me obliquely. The glow from the stage defined one side of his head and gleamed along the side piece of his glasses.

"Windsor," he introduced himself.

"Who's for a wide blue sky-high fling?"

"We are! We're on the wing!"

"I'm sorry to break into your evening." The man spoke the kind of English that is heard only on the cold war propaganda networks, the accent unplaceable but definitely there.

"Don't apologize," I said. "This show had too good a press." I had broken a rule, and didn't care.

I had come here because tomorrow I was going home and I wanted to take away a memory, however trivial, of the New Liberal Germany that people talked so much about. The Neukomödie-theater was said to be the center of fresh youthful gaiety (*Süddeutsche Zeitung*) where the new generation was making its breakthrough to a kind of music that had not been heard before (*Der Spiegel*). No one had mentioned the corn.

"What a pity you are disappointed," murmured the man, "on your last night in Berlin." He glanced down at the stage and then moved his chair back quietly. "Perhaps I can interest you by way of conversation." For a moment I had thought he was leaving, but he had sat down again. His chair was now below one of the little shaded lamps on the wall of the box, so that his face was in shadow.

I wondered who he was.

"Perhaps, Mr. Quiller," he said softly, leaning toward me, "you would care to move your chair closer, so that we can speak quietly." He added: "My name is Pol."

I did not move. "Apart from your name, Herr Pol, I don't know anything about you. I think you are making a mistake. This box was reserved for me exclusively: Number 7. Yours is possibly Number 1. The figures are sometimes confused."

The girls and boys were wheeling about the stage with their arms out like wings, swooping and diving and cleverly missing each other in what the press called an aerial ballet of intricate patterns that bespelled the eye. Now the stage lights went dim and the dancers were seen to be wearing tiny electric lamps on their hands as they wove their way about each other. I was saddened. Even the gay new generation couldn't make its breakthrough without putting on a number that unconsciously resembled an air battle.

Pol said gently: "I came to talk to you here because it is a good place. Better than a café or your hotel. I was not seen coming here, and if you would care to move your chair back we should be completely concealed, in this light."

I said: "You're mistaking me for someone else. Don't oblige me to call the usher and lodge a complaint."

He said: "Your attitude is understandable, so I won't cavil."

I moved my chair back and sat closer to him.

"All right," I said.

"Windsor" was the presently operating code word, given as a name when approaching a contact. The C Group had been in operation since the first of this month, giving us "care," "call," and "cavil." I would have cleared him provisionally on "care" alone, be-

15

cause he knew three things about me: my name was Quiller, my box number was 7, and this was my last night in Berlin. But I had thrown him "call" to get "cavil" simply in the hope that he wasn't a contact at all, but someone who had wandered into the wrong box and used the word "care" by chance.

I didn't want any more contacts, any more work. Six months in this field had left me sickened and I wanted England more than I had ever wanted her before.

It was no go. This was a contact.

Uncivilly I told him to explain how he had known which box I was in.

He said: "I followed you here."

"You didn't." I knew when I was being followed.

"Correct," he said.

So it had been a test for me: he had wanted to know if people could follow me about without my realizing it. I resented the trap.

"We knew that you had reserved this box," he said.

I looked down at the firefly dance on the stage. The music played softly. It took me three or four seconds. I had booked for the show by phone, asking for a box because I didn't want to sit with anyone; half my six months had been spent sitting wedged between people at the trial and I felt contaminated. This reservation had been made in the name of Schultze, so he could have gone right through the list at the box office without finding me. There was only one way.

Between us we set three quick traps and sprung them:

"So you've got access to the box office."

"Yes."

"No go. I used the name Schultze."

"We knew that."

"By tapping my phone."

He said: "Correct."

My leading trap had been set to find out if he were still testing me. He was. Otherwise he would have said, "No, we didn't go to the box office." Instead, he had trapped me back at once with the one word—"Yes"—to see if I'd spring it. I did: with "Schultze." Even then he wouldn't let me off the hook, because I had only gone halfway, telling him that I knew he would have drawn a blank at the box office. That was how they hadn't found me; he wanted me to tell him how they had. He wanted the other half: how had they known about Schultze? So I threw it for him and he took it: "Correct."

I didn't like that word. He'd used it twice. It was a schoolmaster's word. I didn't like being tested. Who did he think I was—a fresh scout just out of the training school?

Down there they'd got off their chests the aerial ballet of intricate patterns that bespelled the eye, and the footlights came on again. Under the applause I said loudly: "I don't like being put through the hoop by an unknown contact right at the bitter end of a mission and I don't like my phone being tapped. How long has it been going on?"

Blandly he said: "You tell me."

The glow from the stage seemed bright after the gloom, and I took a good look at his face. It was a round face and almost featureless. Mud-brown eyes behind schoolboy-type horn-rimmed spectacles with plain glass in them that didn't magnify even by a fraction, but good at their job since they made one bold feature for the blank face. Hair brown. Nothing to go on. If I wanted to recognize this man again I would have to watch him walk. Unnecessary. Tomorrow I'd be in England, therefore to hell with him.

I said quietly (the applause was dying away): "It hasn't been tapped for long or I'd have caught the clicks."

He began talking rapidly and softly with his hands to his face to focus the sound of his voice on my ear alone.

"I was flown out from London this morning with orders to make contact in strict hush. I wasn't allowed to go to your hotel or meet you anywhere in public, so Local Control had a difficult task. Your phone was tapped sometime before noon in the hope that we could find out your program for the day and somehow provide contact for me, and it was most fortunate that we heard you telephone for a box at the Neukomödietheater."

"Played into your hands, like a fool."

I was pleased to see his look of mild pain. I was acting the rebel. Tomorrow I was being let out of school, so tonight I could cheek whom I chose, and he was handy. Also he was a stranger and might be a top kick of some kind very high in the echelon, out here in the field to chuck his weight about incognito. If so I could be saucy and get away with it until he identified himself. The show wasn't turning out so badly after all.

He said: "This is all fully urgent."

It was the big signal, then. "Fully Urgent" was Control's phrase for covering most of the other ones from "Top Secret" through "Action at Once" to "Priority Red."

He could keep it.

"Find someone else," I said. "I'm homeward bound."

I felt better now. The big signal wasn't for monkeying with, and I'd monkeyed.

The words came softly out of his cupped hands:

"KLJ was found dead last night."

It caught me like a blow in the face, and I began sweating immediately. Years of training had kept my eyes and mouth and hands expressionless as the shock of the words hit me, and the body, denied instinctive reaction, has to do something at a time like this; so I sat facing him with calm eyes and a quiet mouth and motionless hands, and felt the sweat coming.

He said: "We want you to take his place."

2 | THE HOOK

I told him they couldn't expect it of me.

He said it was a request, not an order.

Talking was difficult most of the time because the music would break suddenly now and then in a good imitation of the *West Side Story* style, and a word we had pitched against the volume of the orchestra would explode in a gap of silence. It was easier during the two intervals: we locked the door of the box and sat on the carpet with our backs to the balcony, unviewable even from the highest box on the other side of the auditorium; the murmur of the people gave good background cover for our voices.

One thought was lodged in my head like a bullet. KLJ was dead.

I had asked Pol about it and he said: "Floating in the Grunewaldsee." So there was Kenneth Lindsay Jones's place. We all have a place. We know where we were born but not where we shall die. At home, or a mile away at the crossroads, or far across the face of the earth; not knowing it in our sleep, or pitched down on the wet road, or trapped in the wreckage on the mountainside and knowing it only too well. A place for each of us, and there was his, the lake at Grunewald renamed Kenneth Lindsay Jones by virtue of his presence.

We'd lost five men during my time at the Bureau but this one was said to be unkillable.

Pol had told me more because I had asked. "A very long-range shot in the spine from a 9.3 again, as it was with Charington."

Then we stopped talking about KLJ as if he'd never existed. Pol set about stalking me and I let him, sitting with my back to the balcony and listening to the quiet modulated tone that I was already beginning to hate.

"We are highly impressed with the way you have been working on these war crime inquiries. There was no need for secrecy because the matter comes under the terms of the London Agreement, yet you chose to maintain strict hush and we have been told that even the chief of the Z Commission had no knowledge of the man responsible for the arrests. We assume that your reason was to keep in practice."

He waited for confirmation. I enjoyed my silence.

"Further, your operations have been on the periphery of a search area that was opened at the Bureau three weeks ago, on pressure from Paris. No one—now—has more information on the Berlin nucleus of ex-Nazi and neo-Nazi diehards than yourself. This now becomes invaluable to us and so do you."

He gave up waiting for me to help him along, and this was a danger I didn't see until it was much too late. By refusing to answer him even by a grunt, I was letting him keep up a monologue in that soft and modulated tone that never gave pause. And it was hypnotic.

"Of the fifteen war criminals you have indirectly arrested, five as you know were of major status, and we believe that the recent suicides of General Vogler, General Muntz, and Baron von Lüding were provoked by pressure from their own group rather than by the dictates of conscience."

He talked about the three prosecution witnesses found shot dead and facially mutilated. "They were not removed in order to decrease the number of witnesses at the Hannover Trials because there are, as you know, nearly one thousand of them, and the mass of evidence is such that one could remove ninety percent of them and still remain certain of conviction. Those three were murdered *in reprisal,* and we believe that there will follow twelve more unless the Federal police can protect them. In all, fifteen. One for every war criminal convicted. Further, the intention is to dissuade new witnesses from coming forward at the successor trials in Bonn and Nürnberg. They intend by terror tactics to ensure that the Hannover Trial shall be the last of its kind ever held."

I had his accent now, from the "ür" in "Nürnberg." He was a Rhinelander.

He talked about the seventy thousand Nazi refugees and self-exiles living in the German colony in San Caterina, Argentina, among them the Hitler deputy Bormann. "As you know, their Tacuara organization carried out reprisals against the Jewish population following the Eichmann abduction."

I wished he would stop saying "As you know," or better, tell me something I didn't.

"But Zossen is here in Berlin."

He stopped. I knew why. I was hooked.

I said: "Heinrich Zossen?"

"Yes."

A thin man. Pale of face, with dewlaps and a pouchy mouth. Round-shouldered like his Führer. Little blue eyes, the blue of ice. A voice like a reed in a winter wind.

I had last seen him twenty-one years ago, on an August morning when three hundred of them were lined up at the brink of the pit they had been made to dig from the rich earth of the forest of Brücknerwald. The birds had stopped singing when the S.S. staff car drew up and Obergruppenführer Heinrich Zossen got out. I watched him as he walked behind the lines of the three hundred naked men as if inspecting them. He turned and walked back and I watched him. He was a young man for his rank and proud of his uniform. He was not a thug. A thug would have taken a whip from a guard and drawn blood from even these bloodless buttocks for our amusement; he would have pointedly held his nose, reminded that these men had been moved a hundred and thirty miles through the night in sealed cattle trucks, packed ninety to a truck;

he would have taken his revolver and fired the first bullet himself, to lead the fun. He did none of these things. He was an officer. He did worse, and I watched him do it.

A guard shouted as one of the three hundred men broke from the ranks and came toward the Obergruppenführer. He was not riddled where he stood because Zossen had raised his gloved hand, curious to know why the man had left the ranks. He had once been bigger than Zossen; his frame, outlined beneath the skin, was wide at the shoulder; but now he was smaller, because most of the flesh had gone and he looked as if made of paper. This batch, as I knew, had lived for months on acorns, crusts, and rancid water. It would be impossible to judge how long it had been since they had eaten what anyone could call a meal.

The Jew walked up to the Aryan in black and came to a lurching stop. The effort of walking ten yards had brought the breath hissing in his mouth, and his rib cage pulsed beneath the skin that hung from the bones like loose yellow silk. I heard him ask Zossen if it were allowed that they all might sing, for one minute only, a prayer—the Kaddish. The Obergruppenführer did not knock him down for his impudence, as I had expected. He was an officer. He looked at the watch on his wrist, considered a moment, and shook his head. "There is not enough time. The roads are bad and I am due back in Brücknerwald in one hour for luncheon." He signaled his Sturmbannführer and the machine guns opened up.

Heinrich Zossen. I remembered him.

Normally one would keep such a memory to oneself for the sake of decency, but as a leading witness for the prosecution at the 1945 Tribunal, I was obliged to recount this event, among many others. The others were no better, but it was mentioned afterward that throughout my testimony totaling fifteen weeks I spoke calmly and objectively, with one brief lapse. This was when I spoke of Heinrich Zossen. Even now, twenty-one years later, in a Berlin where you could hear the singing from the synagogue rising freely, I was unable, when in a restaurant, to open a menu headed with that word, *Mittagessen*. Luncheon.

Pol was still silent, knowing that he'd played the ace. Zossen was in Berlin.

"Then I hope you get him," I said.

Still silent. He was playing my own game.

"But I think you're wrong. They say he's in Argentina."

Now we both talked and I knew that he knew that he'd won. He said:

"He was seen in Berlin a week ago."

"Who saw him?"

"A witness at the trial."

"I'll talk to him then."

"He fell from the tenth floor of the Witzenhausenhof the day after he had told us."

"Olbricht?"

"Yes."

"He could have been mistaken."

"He knew Zossen well. You know that."

"Is that part of the search area, then? Zossen?"

"It has become part of it."

"So you're roping me in."

"Yes."

"Because you know I'd like to see him on trial. No go. They don't hang them any more." I suddenly said a terrible thing, because I believed Pol was genuine and my guard was down. "Give me a rope, though, give me a rope and ask no questions."

He was silent.

I said: "I'm tired, that's all."

"Of course. After six months' work . . ."

"Don't talk to me like a bloody nurse."

He was silent again. The hum of voices was loudening under the domed roof as the people left the bars and went back to their seats.

"Come on then, Pol. You haven't got long. Finish me off."

He said immediately, as if I'd switched on a tape: "There are thousands of Nazis still living in Germany with false papers and even the Federal intelligence services are riddled with them. The

U.S. Gehlen Bureau quietly released hundreds of Army and S.S. officers from internment when General Heusinger dictated his terms to NATO, and they have since reorganized the German Army, which is now the largest and best equipped in Europe. The German Air Force is at present ahead of the R.A.F. in striking power. The German General Staff has made secret non-NATO deals with Spain, Portugal, Egypt, and African countries and established its own bases with ground-to-ground missiles. Scores of Hitler's officers have returned to power and influence in both civil and military key positions, and their posts were granted them in the full knowledge of their past activities. In the General Staff itself there is a military microcosm of dedicated Nazis, a hard core prepared for an explosive expansion when the opportunity comes. If—"

"Pol," I said, "did the Bureau give you this stuff?"

"I am an executive, like yourself, not an administrator."

"If I decided—and I haven't—to take over this new operation without even a day's break, I'd have to be convinced of their argument. It would take days. I think the GGS is no more likely to make a war than the Ku Klux Klan."

"Let me remind you how the U.S. prosecutor put it at the Nürnberg Tribunal: 'German militarism will tie itself to *any* new creed in order to regain the power of making war.' There are new creeds emerging now in Egypt, China, Cuba. Further, they realize the huge potential of the GGS and its value as an ally, given the right ground: a world on the brink."

"You can't start war without people."

"People never start wars. Politicians and generals start them. As long as ten years ago—only ten years after the bloodshed stopped—there was a rally of ex-Nazi soldiers in honor of Kesselring. The people protested but the police pushed them back and kept order."

"The people are still protesting, by means of the trials."

"And now the trials are becoming more and more difficult.

Convicted war criminals are no longer hanged, but witnesses are being shot. The tide is on the turn."

I sat with my eyes shut. The auditorium had gone dark. Music was playing. A girl sang.

Pol was silent. He knew that in persuasion one must pause, so that the subject is given time to dwell.

"Political polemics," I said wearily. "Keep them. Shove them down the next man's throat."

His silence was disapproving.

"I don't claim, Pol, to have my finger on the pulse of the human condition or to know what future mankind has, if it has any. And I'm tired. You chose the wrong box, just as I told you in the beginning."

He was moving about and I opened my eyes. From somewhere he'd taken a plastic briefcase. It must have been under his jacket. I would have seen it before, otherwise. He put it on my knees.

"I am to leave this with you," was all he said.

I let it rest there without touching it.

"Damn your impudence, Pol."

"We have arranged a cover man for you," he said softly, "and a front."

"I don't want a cover."

"What happens if you get into a corner?"

"I'll get out again."

"You know the risks, Quiller."

"Did KLJ use a cover man?"

"Yes, but it is difficult to cover anyone from a long-range shot."

"That's the way they'll get me if it comes to it. No cover, Pol. And don't post one without my knowing. I'm going in alone."

A pulse had begun beating in my leg, the onset of cramp. I moved and the briefcase slid off my knees. I left it where it fell. Pol said softly as the music broke:

"There are two people you can trust—"

"No people."

"An American, Frank Brand, and a young German, Lanz Hengel. They—"

"Keep them clear of me."

"You have a link man—"

"Keep him clear."

"It is myself. I am your link man."

"Keep clear of me then."

If I were going in, it had to be on my terms. They couldn't expect it of me and they shouldn't have sent this man Pol to hook me like this. They were bastards. Charington dead—get another man. KLJ dead—get another man. Who would they get after me? Six months hard, now this, and because of expedience, because I was handy. And they had the hook. "There's only one way to persuade him," they'd said, standing around the desk in that London room with the Lowrie and the smell of polish. "Tell him someone has seen Zossen in Berlin." And they'd lit a cigarette and sent for Pol.

I didn't care whether the monologue about a renascent Nazi group was genuine or not. Given Zossen I needed no further blandishments. They'd wasted my time.

The cramp was beginning so I crawled on my hands and knees to the back of the box and got into the chair as if I'd just come in again after the interval. Pol did the same, brushing his hands carefully across the knees of his trousers. I sat with my eyes shut, thinking.

Now that I'd stopped resenting him and made the decision, I could admit that it was my own fault. For years I'd operated in strict hush, as I'd been trained to do; so when they seconded me to liaise with the Federal Z Commission and supply the Hannover Tribunal with bodies for trial, I hadn't seen much point in coming into the open air. If I had, my face would have become, in those six months, the most recognizable feature ever to have spanned the crossed hairs of a telescopic rifle-sight. That wouldn't have worried me because I'd moved between Berlin and Hannover and back with a constant cover of six men, like a pocket president. But my insistence on secrecy had got me on this hook. After six months I knew Berlin like my face, yet my face was unknown in Berlin.

No wonder they'd come for me.

For a while Pol must have thought I'd refuse. Then he knew it was going to be all right, and had put the briefcase on my knees. It would contain all the information they could give me, all the names, suspects, dossiers, leads and theories they could cull from the whole of the Bureau files, a complete and exhaustive breakdown on the field. But they'd come for me because I knew even more.

"Pol," I said.

He was sitting with his arms folded, head tilted, watching the show. His head tilted the other way, toward me.

I said: "Tell them not to try tapping my phone again. I want to be able to know that if I hear any clicks, it's the adverse party doing it."

"Very well."

"No cover."

"Noted."

"Communication Post and Bourse."

"Available."

When the stage began filling and the music was loud, I asked him for his photo and he gave it to me. The zip on the briefcase was the interlocking plastic flange type and opened silently. Inside was the folder with the black cover. It was the memorandum. Between the typed lines was written, invisibly, my future.

In detail it gave specific outline to the manner of my life. It made no mention of the possible manner of my death. It was thus a highly personal document, and on the cover was a single letter: Q.

I put the photograph in and shut the case.

3 | SNOW

The snow had stopped. It had been packed into ice by the tires, and the traffic was slow and quiet. Halfway along the Kurfürstenstrasse a street bollard lay smashed and they were towing the car clear; rusty water steamed as it poured from the radiator. Above the roofs the sky was black and the stars close. It was easy to see tonight that the earth was a star too, adrift in a void; a fur collar gave little protection against the thought.

I had left the box a minute before Pol so that when he went down the main staircase in the throng he couldn't see me. I had kept back by the wall on the balcony to get a good look at his face in the mirror above the stairs. I compared it with his photograph, and asked for a plain envelope on my way past the box office. In the street I put the photograph inside and addressed it to Radio Eurosound, posting it, unstamped, in the box at the curbside.

It was fifteen minutes' walk to my hotel on dry pavements. Tonight it took just short of thirty. The ice crackled underfoot. Only four of my cover men were within sight, picking me up at the Neukomödietheater and tailing at a distance. They worked well but they were useless because the system was useless. Once inside a theater you were meant to be safe, but Pol could easily have been one of the adverse party and slipped a knife into me and no one the wiser. Useless.

There were fresh placards along the Bülowstrasse, and I saw

Peters' name, and bought a late edition. Ewald Peters, Chancellor Erhard's chief personal security man. Only last month he'd been in London, protection for the Chancellor in case anyone threw a tomato. Now they'd arrested him. Charge: mass murder of Jews. He was a senior official in the Federal Kriminalpolizei and responsible for the security of the Chancellor, the President of the Republic, and visiting statesmen in Bonn. How much had Erhard known? Probably nothing. He'd resisted pressure recently at the Party Congress, insisting on continuing the trials and refusing the plea for an amnesty that would release a score of Nazis from the cells. If he'd suspected his chief bodyguard, he'd have turned the man over right away.

It was the Z Commission who'd nabbed Peters. I admired them for that—they were more bulldog than dachshund. There was already a lot of unrest inside the department because their job was exclusively to hunt down the Nazi remnant, and since there were several Nazis in the hierarchy of their own section they risked losing promotion with every arrest they made. A very odd way to run an *Eisenbahn*.

Yesterday they'd got Hans Krueger, West German Minister for Refugees. Charge: serving as a judge at a "special" Nazi court in Poland. In a few days' time there'd be a new name on the placards, because the Z Polizei were just now tying up the loose ends. Franz Röhm, Secretary of the Road Safety Committee. It had taken me three weeks to find him. I was pleased with that one because suicide was among my subjects and I knew Röhm would kick a chair from under him any day now. I didn't hold with capital punishment; it had been abolished in West Germany since 1949, and that was good; but these men were infectious and there was one thing worse than that they should hang: it was that they should live, and infect others.

The snow crackled under my feet.

I turned into the north end of the Kreuzberg Garten and passed the fountain; it was a frozen ice cake. Another dozen yards and there was some shadow cast by shrubs, and I melted, waiting.

When the first one came past, I moved into the light of the lamps and stopped him, saying in German:

"For Local Control, please. I've met Pol. Spelt P-O-L. From now on they're to call off all cover, fully urgent. They can find me Post and Bourse."

He lit the cigarette I'd put between my lips.

"I shall have to confirm before I leave."

"The sooner the better," I said. "The others can stay until you've confirmed. Then call them off. I want a clear field from midnight."

I thanked him for the light and walked on, flicking the cigarette away as soon as there was a chance. Nearing the hotel through the Schönerlinderstrasse where the pavement was being cleared of snow, I heard an airliner go surging up from the Tempelhof less than a mile away, and turned to watch its lights.

In the morning I would have to cancel my reservation on Lufthansa 174, because it was written between the lines of the thrice-accursed memorandum that I must stay.

Naumann: the snowman. Sickert: sick at heart. Kalt: cold. Helldorf: held off. Kielmann: kill a man. Hansnig: hands. Edsel: easily. Shuffle.

Helldorf. Sickert. Kalt. Naumann. Kielmann. Edsel. Hansnig.

Try it.

I held off, sick at heart to see the cold snowman kill a man so easily with his hands.

There were forty-odd names on a single sheet of the memorandum, each one a possible contact of Heinrich Zossen. In half an hour they were locked in my memory and the sheet was added to the pile for burning. My habit was to travel light; by morning the complete memorandum would be cremated.

A mental note: keyword "whale." Tell Control to turn the heat off the big fish so that they relaxed their vigilance while I got within range.

It was only the smaller fish I'd netted so far. They'd sent KLJ after the big ones and now he was dead. The big ones were people like the Hitler deputy Bormann, and Mueller, and General von Rittmeister. They'd got out of Berlin under fire from the Russian batteries in '45, a whole gang of them running for Obersalzberg and beyond, while their Führer's short round-shouldered carcass was smothered in a petrol-soaked rag and set alight. Some of them had taken off in Himmler's four-motor plane from the *Flughafen* a mile from here through a dawn sky dark with smoke. I could see the runway lights from this window now.

I went across to it. Outside, the night was still and the city frozen in sleep. The present and the past lay buried under the snow. What made us rake like this among the ashes of that distant hell after twenty years? They said it was to help a nation to its feet. The new young Germany had heard too many tales of the war that had raged above its unborn head, and wanted to know the truth, and face it and then forget. That was the reason.

It wasn't mine.

"Have we a minute," they said, "to sing a prayer?" He shook his head.

My breath made a bloom on the window's glass. The room was too hot, so I turned the radiators off, and then worked for another hour. With half the memorandum shuffled, linked, and recorded in my mind, I left the hotel and walked on the snow to clear my lungs for sleep. The street was empty.

Even in the instant of deciding I'd take over from KLJ, the main plan had presented itself to me, just as a player sometimes gets an overall vision of the board before he makes his gambit. Therefore I'd told Pol: "I'm going in alone." Because it had to be a fast operation or nothing, a *Blitzkrieg* on their own terms. I could stick in this city another month, no more. In a month I'd have to find him or get out.

There were two ways to do it: the slow and the quick. The slow way was to flush those men one by one—Helldorf, Sickert, Kalt and the whole forty-odd of them—in the hope that they'd lead me to Zossen. Pol had played too fair with me, calling Zossen no more than "a part of the search area." The first quick reading of the memorandum told me that Zossen was the *whole* of the area. Knock him down and the rest would skittle over. To get to him by first calling on those forty-odd contacts would bring a great deal into the light, and that was what the Bureau wanted. It was the slow way. But the quick way would get the same result. Go straight to Zossen and strike.

The quick way was to reverse the order of things. To find one man among three and a half million I must let him find me. Let him know I was here and here to get him. Draw his fire, so that he'd show himself. Then try to finish him off before he finished me. Hope for an overkill.

So I'd told Pol I must work alone. The only way was the quick way and I didn't want it cluttered up with a motley crew of cover men who'd trip me and get killed in the process.

The snow lay shimmering under the lamps. There'd been another light fall while I'd been working on the memorandum and the pavement was covered again. It had long gone midnight and the street was empty. After six months of cover protection I was alone; not in any doorway nor in any shadow did a man stand. Control had got my signal and called them off.

As I walked back to the hotel the only tracks in the snow were my own.

4 | THE WALL

"Your occupation, Heer Stroebling?"

"Florist."

He blew his nose, taking his time about it so that we could admire the white silk handkerchief. A flower was in the lapel of the dark jacket. The legs were casually crossed in the pin-stripe trousers and the shoes shone.

"You are a florist?"

"I direct a chain of shops."

"Is that why you wear a flower in your buttonhole?"

"I always wear a flower."

Someone tittered.

The light was bleak in the tall cold windows. The heating was full on but many still wore their overcoats, as if in need of comfort.

Another objection: personal comment on appearance of accused. Overruled: not customary to enter this court dressed as if for a festive occasion, therefore reason sought.

I watched the spectators particularly. I knew who the accused were. I didn't know who the spectators were. Some were the wives of the accused and had come here with them, for most of the accused were on bail and free to go home at the end of the session. There were others in the gallery who came and went alone, hunched into their coats, their eyes for no one. A few were women.

One girl had come in late this morning and I had noticed her. She was good-looking but I hadn't noticed her because of that.

"Usher!"

A man was trying to slip out of the doors, and on the presiding judge's cry an usher stopped him.

"Where are you going, counsel?"

"I am expecting a message, Herr Richter."

"You must not leave the court. I've told you before."

"It's a message to do with my clients, Herr—"

"Resume your place."

Both spoke wearily, repeating the formula. It was one of the recognized nuisance-tactics designed to wear down the patience of the court: a defense counsel would try to slip out unnoticed, so that later an appeal could be made under the Federal law on the grounds that some of the accused were technically unrepresented during a part of the hearing, their counsel being absent.

Procedural objections were also frequent. In the streets outside, the tabloids militated against this trial and all war crime trials, while inside the court there were attempts at every turn to make a farce of the proceedings. They were totally unsuccessful. The presiding judge had the patience of a cat, and the legal and lay panel was disciplined by it.

I watched the spectators, only half-listening to the examination.

"Will you please tell us what your responsibility was at the camp, Herr Stroebling?"

He considered the question. Neat, silver-haired, professional-looking, his eyes calm behind heavy black-framed glasses, you'd take him for a top-ranking medical man and trust him with your life.

"To maintain calm, order, and, of course, cleanliness."

"And your special duties?"

"I had no special duties."

"Evidence has been given that your special duty was to select men, women, and children for the gas chambers as they were unloaded from the cattle trucks." It was the counsel for the prosecution speaking now: a young man with a face hollowed by months of sifting the reports whose every sheet recorded the unimaginable. The two counsels for the prosecution had been chosen for their youth, so that the new Germany could demand the account of the old. "It is claimed by an established eyewitness that while ordering the selection of disabled deportees for the gas chambers, you took a crutch from a cripple and beat him to death with it because he wouldn't hurry to the chambers."

"I know nothing of that."

"You cannot claim to *know nothing*. You can say that you did this thing, or that you didn't. You cannot just *forget*."

Was it a camellia or a gardenia in the buttonhole? I couldn't see from where I sat.

"It was twenty years ago."

"It was twenty years ago for the witness, too, but he hasn't forgotten."

I watched the spectators. The voices droned.

"You say these people went willingly into the gas chambers on that occasion?"

"Yes. We had told them they were delousing rooms."

"So they left all their clothes in the changing room, hanging on pegs, and followed one another into the gas chambers, peacefully?"

"Yes. There was no persuasion."

"But the evidence has it that some of them knew they were going to die. Several women left their babies hidden under the clothes in the changing room, hoping to save them. The evidence has it that you personally, Herr Stroebling, led a hunt for such infants, and that you spitted them on bayonets when they were found."

It was too warm in here, too wearisome to lie.

"They were only Jews, I keep telling you."

A man among the spectators, an official of some sort with a peaked cap, broke down, and his sobs were embarrassing; an usher led him out. It was common enough.

The good-looking girl in the black Russian hat watched him go.

She never looked in my direction so I couldn't see her expression. She stared mostly at the accused, with her face pale.

The voices droned.

". . . But I was given full and legal power, absolute power to treat these prisoners as I thought right!"

"And you thought it right to mutilate the body of this ten-year-old boy with every instrument of torture known to man, for the amusement of your friends?"

"For their instruction! They were not my friends, they were my junior officers, some of them just out of training college! They had to be hardened, and I had explicit orders to harden them!"

A woman was moaning, rocking on the bench, moaning with anger, her teeth chattering, staring at the accused. She was led from the court on the judge's instruction. I had not ever seen, in six months, a woman sob. It was always the men. The women moaned or cried out in their anger.

". . . It was ordered me by Standartenführer Goetz!"

"He is not here to confirm that."

(No. He was still in Argentina, where the Bonn Ministry of Justice had asked for his extradition. He was also in my memory, out of the burned memorandum. Goetz, the goiter.)

". . . And all the time you were on these 'administrative duties,' Herr Stroebling, you say you did not know of any deaths taking place among your prisoners?"

A fingernail now bitten to the quick.

"A few. I knew of a few."

"A few? Out of three million five hundred thousand done to death at this single camp? A few?"

The young prosecutor was drinking water again. Three times they'd refilled the glass jug. He drank in gulps, breathing as if he'd been running hard. All the time he drank he didn't take his eyes from the accused.

I watched the spectators, but there was no one I could recognize. Sometimes these people, just as with ordinary human people, returned to the scene of their crime, reenacted in these places by verbal witness and film projected onto the roll-up screens. I'd got five of them that way.

But it was one man I wanted now, out of all this city. Zossen. Of the many faces in my memory, I could recall only a dozen that I'd seen in that man's company; of that dozen, none was here.

Dark came before the session ended. I waited my turn at the doors. People left this place looking drugged, as if awakening from a nightmare under anesthesia. I knew that three of the lay jury were under the constant observation of their doctors to avert a breakdown before the trial ended.

They shuffled into the vault of the main hall. The girl in the black fur hat was ahead of me. The big doors were fastened wide open, framing a rainbow of colors on the snowy street. The air tasted of metal in the mouth. I began walking. The others had nearly all turned in the other direction, toward the interurban stop. There were only three people anywhere near me: a man signaling a taxi, a man going into the pharmacy next to the hall we had left, and the girl in the fur hat.

Directly facing the steps of the Neustadthalle is a narrow street forming a T-section with the Wittenaustrasse, along which I was walking. There are no standards for the lamps at this place: they're suspended from overhead cables. There is a stretch of blank wall for twenty yards, concealing a cemetery.

They missed.

The car came from the narrow street and swung in a curve to smash the rear end against the wall so close that brick dust stung my face as I threw myself clear and fell, rolling at once to get my prone body in line with the car feet-first in case they risked the sound of a shot. None came. I heard the diminishing exhaust-note and the strange wailing of the girl. I got up and found her in an odd crouch against the wall, shivering and staring at the distant car. I hadn't troubled to get the number: it would have false plates.

I called in German: "Are you hurt?"

There was no telling what she was saying; it sounded like soft cursing; she stared after the car; she didn't even hear me. There was no snow on her coat; she hadn't fallen. A great gouge ran along the wall, and brick dust and chippings colored the snow.

No one had come up. You heard it all the time in this weather, cars coming unstuck. This one had slid off course or it would have been dead on target, to pin me and drag me along the wall like a paintbrush dipped in red. The operation needed judgment, but was easier than it looked. I'd done it with sandbags in training, because we were required to know the mechanics of it in case we were ever the target. It went: get up speed as far away as feasible, then slip the clutch with the gear still in low and go in silently, freewheeling until you're lined up at ten or fifteen degrees with the wall and a few yards to the rear of target. Then clutch in and gun up hard to get the back end round in a power-slide that brings the target between the rear wing and the wall. Keep the foot down and get clear.

I'd burst four sandbags out of five. It wasn't the training that saved me, but the snow.

She had said something intelligible.

"What?" I asked.

"They were trying to kill me," she said. She spoke brittle Berliner German. I assumed that normally her voice would be less harsh than now.

"Really?" I said. She was walking—half running—along the pavement. She obviously hadn't meant to say that. When I caught up with her she swung round like a slim blond tiger and stood her ground. A man sized us up and said:

"Can I help you, Fräulein?"

She didn't look at him, but stared at me. "No." The man went away. She faced me with a cat's undivertibility.

"I'm not one of them, Fräulein Windsor." We both stood perfectly still.

"Who are you?"

"Not one of them."

"Leave me alone." The pupils still almost filled the blue, dilated in anger.

"Would you care for me to call a cab?" She hadn't taken "Windsor" but I persisted because she was shocked and might not have got it.

"I'll walk." No go with the C Group either. It was a thin bid anyway: the bastards had been after me all right, but she believed they'd been after her, which could mean that she was with the Bureau. She wasn't, because she didn't respond. The Z Commission used several women; she might be one of them.

She was backing from me, hands in the pockets of her military-style coat. Before she could slip me, I took a long shot. "They had no more luck this time than the last, did they?"

She stood still again, eyes narrow. "Who are you?"

It had come off. They'd tried before. The first time they try, you don't always realize it, especially if it's meant to look like an accident. The second time, you get that certain feeling. She had it now.

"Let's have a drink," I said. "Get the brick dust out of our mouths." I didn't say it in my best German because a strong English accent would help to disarm her; that car was Nazi, because it had tried to kill me; she must know it was Nazi because she believed it had tried to kill her; there couldn't be many Nazis with an English accent as natural as mine. She said:

"What is your name?"

"You wouldn't know it. There's a bar over there."

She had great powers of stillness. Her eyes didn't blink once. When she had finished inspecting me, she said:

"We shall talk where it's safe, at my flat."

Twice on the way she pressed herself into a shop entrance when she heard a car come close and each time I walked on, because if they were going to try again I didn't want her to be too near me; each time, I turned to watch the car in case it was necessary to jump clear.

It was a mile to her flat, and I busied myself with the question all the time: how had they got on to me so soon? The answers weren't satisfactory, any of them. They might have suspected me because of my cover men, who were less concerned with keeping out of sight than with watching me and anyone who came near me. They might even have known that I was due out of here on the London plane today, and decided that if I were going to stay I wasn't going to stay alive. They might have seen me going into the Neustadt-halle here in Berlin this morning instead of flying to the court in Hannover as usual, and decided that I was showing up in too many wrong places. One thing I knew: I hadn't been followed anywhere. I know when I'm being followed.

The interesting thing was that unless that car had been simply an isolated murder patrol out for a killing to keep its hand in, the orders to get me had come from on high. So I wasn't going to have to stick my neck out to draw their fire: it was already drawn. Within twenty-four hours of my decision to hunt Zossen, Zossen was hunting me.

5 PHÖNIX

Distrusting me in the open street, she was prepared to trust me in the more dangerous confines of her flat, and I assumed there was someone there to protect her.

It was a five-year-old blue Oberschwaben wolfhound, a killer. Once inside the room I kept still. It stood with its head low and its great hindquarters braced for a leap, it jaws slightly parted but soundless. Its eyes were on my throat.

I'd seen them at Belsen and Dachau. They would kill an Alsatian of equal age and weight, given ten minutes on mountain ground. I had seen them kill men.

The girl took off her coat without hurry, so that I should get the message. This would have been clear even to anyone without experience of the breed: if I lifted my hand suddenly in the girl's direction by one inch I'd be dead meat. I kept my arms folded and my face toward the dog. There was no fear-odor on me to provoke it, because I knew it wouldn't attack unless she ordered it.

She said at last, quietly, "Easy, Jürgen. Easy."

It backed from me and I knew that I could move.

"Police-trained," I said.

"Yes." She stood inspecting me, as she had in the street. She was thin, with the hard lines of her body unsoftened by the black polo sweater and slacks; and she stood arrogantly, her hair like a gold helmet. In her stance and her brittle voice there was evident the de-

41

fenselessness that you mark in a man with a gun: he shows it is all he has. She had the dog.

"You still don't trust me," I said. She had told the dog "Easy," not "Friend." If ever I came in here alone, by this door, he'd bring me down in the instant, though he had seen me here before and in her company.

"What will you drink?" she asked me.

"Whatever you're having." I took a second look around. Black everywhere, with hard lines: black Skai furniture with sharp angles, a rank of harsh abstracts and a moody Klee, a pair of boar's tusks mounted on ebony. She brought my Scotch and said:

"I don't trust anyone."

I'd been wrong. Her voice was no less harsh now than it had been after the shock in the street.

"I'm not surprised," I said. "How did they try to kill you the first time?"

"I was in a crowd at a trolley-stop."

"Someone pushed."

"Yes. Just as the trolley was coming. It pulled up in time. Are you with the Z Commission?"

"What's the Z Commission?"

She said nothing, turning away. Jürgen watched her and watched me. I said: "You're too young, Fräulein Lindt, to have seen anything of the war." She turned, swung a glance around the room and saw the envelope, ripped open, on the desk. FRÄULEIN INGA LINDT. "So why do you go to the Neustadthalle?"

Her lithe hips swung and she came halfway toward me and stopped. I was suddenly aware that there was no scent on her or in the room. She stood very still. "Are you prepared to show me your papers?"

I gave her my passport. Quiller. NATO representative for the Red Cross. Scars, groin and left arm. Only two frontier endorsements, Spain and Portugal. We never like it to be thought we're widely traveled and therefore experienced.

"Thank you, Herr Quiller." She looked more relaxed. It seemed she didn't know there was one thing that could lie better than a camera, and that was a passport. I said:

"I'm trying to trace refugees whose relatives have died in England. Some of them have been called as witnesses, so I go to the courts to find them." I didn't think she was listening. She came closer and stared at me.

"You're English. As an Englishman, what do you think of Adolf Hitler?"

"Bit of a fidget."

Her long mouth tightened in contempt. "The English were so safe on their little island. They never saw anything happen."

"No." The one in the groin had been done at Dachau.

"Do you think he is a genius?" she asked me angrily.

"Yes." ("Is" noted.)

"*That* man?"

"An evil genius."

She seemed more satisfied with me. I was beginning to understand. The "is" was the biggest clue. She was living in the past.

I am a bad judge of age in people. The most I could do here was to allow for certain facts: a girl who deliberately watched mass-murder trials, who believed that someone had twice tried to kill her, who kept a wolfhound to protect her, and who showed signs of fierce pent emotion would look older than her age. She looked thirty.

"When will people understand," she said in the strange wail I'd heard against the wall in the street, "that he's got to be blotted out, right out, so that he doesn't *exist* any more?"

There'd been a lot of women like this, ever since Mitford. Now they were dying off but you still came across a few. This one had reached the stage of the obsessional love-hate relationship that presages final rejection: she still had leanings, and had to deal with them by voicing them, even to strangers. She had to get assurance from as many people as possible that she was on the right track now.

"The way to blot him out," I said, "is not to think of him at all. Nobody dies until the last lover stops loving him."

Then her face puckered and she began shaking, and it all came out, beginning with a lot of things like, "No one can understand" and "With me it's different" and "You don't know what it's like," while I quietly sat down on a black futuristic chair and watched her until she brought out the cold hard facts.

"I was in the Bunker." She sat crouched on the floor with her lean shoulders against a chair, spent before she began.

"The Führerbunker?"

"Yes." After the first sip she hadn't touched her drink.

"When?"

She looked blank. "Don't you know when?"

I said: "I don't mean the date. I mean at the beginning, the end, or all the time?"

"All the time."

"How old were you then?"

"I was nine."

"A child."

"Yes."

Her tone had dulled. The answers were so automatic that I suspected she must have given them often before under psychoanalysis. She crouched with her eyes shut. I went on slipping questions in until she took over; it was the classic approach and she was versed in it.

"My mother was a nurse on the special medical staff. With the Goebbels family, there were seven of us in the Bunker—children, I mean—and we didn't have much to do with the grown-ups. But I liked Uncle Hermann and he used to give me things, medals and things."

Hermann Fegelein, of the S.S.

"I saw them bring him in. He had left the Bunker and they brought him back. I heard Hitler shouting at him, then they took him into the Chancellery garden and shot him and I didn't even cry. It was too much for crying. I kept asking my mother why they'd killed poor Uncle Hermann, and she said he'd been wicked. It was the first time I understood what death was: it meant that

44

people went away and you never saw them again. Then the nightmare started and everything began going to pieces inside me. The grown-ups were acting strangely and I used to hide in cupboards and listen in the passages because I was desperate to know what was happening to everyone. At one time I heard a shot and later Frau Junge told me that the Führer was dead; of course I didn't believe her: he was a god to me, to all of us; but there was the smell of burning, in the garden, and one of the Escorts found me and sent me back where I belonged. But I didn't belong anywhere now. Even my mother was strange to me. Even my mother."

The first self-pity had passed and she spoke without emotion, sitting hunched with her arms across her knees, her body as black and angular as the chair. Her gold hair made the only softness in the room.

"The ground began shaking and people said there were Russian soldiers coming. The whole Bunker shook and there was nowhere to run. I stayed with the Goebbels children because the grown-ups frightened me now, but then my mother took me away from them and I never saw them again. I knew they were dead. I didn't know for a long time afterward that it was my mother who had given them the capsules. Of course it was on the orders of Frau Goebbels. There were six of them. Six children."

She opened her eyes but didn't look at me. The wolfhound watched her, worried by the pain in her voice. "The grown-ups frightened me and now even the children had gone. I didn't know what to do. Once I ran to Uncle Guenther when I saw him standing alone at the end of a passage but he told me to go away. There was nowhere to go. Then I saw Goebbels and his wife come into the passage and walk past Uncle Guenther, who had a big can in his hand. I could smell petrol. When I heard the shots from the garden I screamed, but Uncle Guenther didn't even hear me—he simply went out to the garden. I didn't understand anything any more."

Guenther Schwaegermann had been Goebbels' adjutant. His orders had been to smother the bodies in petrol and cremate them.

"That night my mother took me away. We were with a lot of

other people. The ground was shaking and the whole sky was red. There were four women in our party; one of them was the cook. She kept running ahead and the others kept pulling her back, because the Russians were shelling heavily and the whole length of the Friedrichstrasse was on fire. We got as far as the Weidendammer Bridge before I fainted; but I can remember water, and the smell of smoke."

She got to her feet so suddenly that the dog gave a low bark. The curtains were not drawn across the windows and the glow from the street lit her face as she stared down.

I waited, and went on waiting. I didn't move, even to ease the tension in my legs, because I knew the dog was on edge because of her voice. She was statue-still, her thin arms hanging loose from the shoulder, her head forward to stare at the scene below the window that she wasn't seeing.

"That was when the rot set in . . . in the Bunker. When they took Uncle Hermann out and shot him, my own life was altered, in that minute. When the grown-ups began to frighten me with their strangeness I ran back to the only people I could understand—the children. Then they were taken away from me and I knew they were dead too. With nowhere to run next, I felt the whole of the earth moving under my feet, and I knew that the soldiers were coming. But there had to be something I could reach for and trust in. Not my mother, because she was like the other grown-ups, strange and tormented, and I'd seen her coming out of that room where the children were, and knew what had happened. Only someone very powerful could help me now, someone who could never die and who would always be there to help. The only god I had ever been told about was the Führer."

Suddenly she was looking down at me, and because of the angle of the light from the street, the lower part of her face shadowed her eyes and I couldn't see their expression. She said:

"It's called a trauma, isn't it? A psychic injury setting up a neurosis."

It seemed she really wanted an answer, so I said:

46

"I prefer the simpler phrase you used."

"What was that?"

"The rot setting in."

"It's the same thing."

"But a different attitude. The thing is to keep your feet on the ground instead of up on a couch."

"I don't go to psychiatrists any more."

"Then you're the only one in all Berlin who doesn't."

"I tried them."

"Gave them up?"

"Yes."

"Now you go to the Neustadthalle instead."

"Do you know why?"

"To rake the muck with the rest of us, knowing that it's *his* muck. The only successful cure for alcoholism is the nausea drug that teaches you that you can't go on loving something that makes you sick."

I had to be careful not to touch on the question that would have to be answered before I left here. I wanted her to tell me without being asked.

"You understand me very well," she said.

"It's not a very complex situation."

She came and stood over me. She had a way of standing bullfighter-fashion in the black slacks, legs straight, buttocks tucked flat and thighs thrust forward, the hard line of her body curved and tensioned like a bow. In a more feminine woman it would have been provocative; with her it suggested challenge.

"Why did you come here?" she asked me.

"It was an alternative."

"To what?"

"Going to the police."

Her eyes narrowed to slits of light blue under the lids.

"The police?"

"I was a witness to an attempted murder. It was my duty to make an immediate report."

"Why didn't you?"

"Two reasons. You might have been suffering under delusions. It could have been what it looked like: an accident caused by a skid. Also I'm English and in England we tend to trot out our troubles to the nearest policeman because that's what he's there for and we know who he is. In your country you don't. I had to bear that in mind."

"You don't trust our police?"

"I'm certain they're a fine body of men, but yesterday they arrested one of their highest officials on a mass-murder charge—the Chancellor's chief security man. It shows their strength. And their weakness." I stood up and found my glass. It was empty and she took it from me.

"You haven't explained why you came here."

"Again, it was an alternative. I suggested a bar. You suggested here."

"I wanted to talk to you."

"To someone. Anyone."

"Yes. It was a shock. Did you think I hadn't any friends?"

"I still think you haven't. People with friends don't want to talk to strangers." She gave me another drink and her face looked bleak. The arrogance had suddenly gone. I added: "The silliest people can't move for friends. You see them at parties all over the place."

Her body had gone slack. "You made it easy to talk to you. I must have sounded a little hysterical. Do you dismiss me as a psychopath with a persecution complex?"

"Hardly. Someone's just tried to kill you a second time and you didn't even mention it."

"There's nothing to say about it."

But I still had to get that question answered before I left. She didn't dodge it. She didn't even see that I must want to know.

Suddenly it came. "They've got their reasons."

"They?"

"The Nazi group."

"The Nazis have reasons for exterminating someone who's half in love with Hitler?"

"Must you put it like that?"

"Obsessed with the image of a dead god."

Her shoulders were still slack. The defiance was over. The catharsis of the confessional had left her exhausted. She said almost without interest: "I joined their group when I was just out of college. They call it Phönix. It was a foster parent to me because my mother never got to the other side of the Weidendammer Bridge that night. A piece of shrapnel hit her. Then I began growing up, and two or three years ago I defected and left the group. Not suddenly—I just stopped going to that house. They found me and tried to make me go back, because I knew too much. I knew what people had left the Führerbunker alive, and where some of them went. I know where Bormann is now. I refused to go back but I swore on—on something they keep there that I would never talk. Either they think I've talked, or there's a new man there, or a new policy, because there was the trolley-stop incident a month ago, and the car tonight."

I finished my drink. I was going.

"Why do we have such an urge to do something we know we mustn't?" she asked suddenly.

"It's our friend the id. Wants to drive wild, hates the brakes. But keep them on. If it gets difficult, talk to a tape and then burn it. Or talk to Jürgen. But don't talk to strangers any more. You don't know where they'll go when they leave here. If it's straight to the CIA Office or some anti-Nazi organization they won't stage any more accidents—they'll be up here within the hour and you can't rely on Jürgen because he's not bulletproof."

I moved for the door and the wolfhound was on its feet.

"Should I leave Berlin?" she asked wearily.

"It would be safer."

She opened the door for me. Our eyes met and I saw the struggle she was putting up for her pride's sake. She lost.

"You're . . . not with CIA, or anyone?"

49

I said no. "But I could be. Don't forget it. Don't pick up strangers. You never know where they've been."

The street was icy after the close heat of the flat and I walked quickly. Snow got into the sides of my shoes and my breath clouded against my face. I thought about her all the time, and believed that what I had done was right. If there were any doubts they were automatically dismissed when, somewhere along the Unter den Eichen, I knew that I was being followed.

6 | QUOTA

Austrian Union: 293¼. Plus ¼.
BMB Rubber: 106. Plus 1.
Bertram-Rand: 995¾. Minus 5¼.
Cinati: 185½. Plus 1½.
Crowther Development: 344. Plus 6¼.
D.R. Mining: 73. Minus 2.

Just before the corner of the Unter den Eichen and the Albrechtstrasse, I had walked at the same gait but with longer strides so that the spurt didn't show. The first cover down the Albrechtstrasse was a parked beer truck, and I stood against its offside and used the long-stemmed driving mirror to watch the corner. When he was past the truck, hurrying now, I crossed the street and bought an evening edition of *Die Leute* and carried it half-opened to alter the image. After a while he tracked back, and I watched him take quick checks before trying the bar, the pharmacy, and the news agent's where I'd bought the paper.

He was worried now and stood on the pavement stamping his feet as if they were cold. It was frustration. Then he got going again, and we rounded the whole of the Steglitz block before he gave up and made for a beerhouse in the Schöneberg area. I held off for fifteen minutes but he never looked at his watch and no one turned up, so I went in and sat down at his table and said:

"If I see you again I'll put such a blast through to Local that you'll end up washing the stairs."

He looked even younger than he was. He wouldn't even trust himself to speak until my beer came because he was so frustrated. Then he said:

"You know what happened to KLJ."

"It isn't going to happen to me."

"He was a damned good man." It sounded even more emphatic in German. He was angry about that death. His name was Hengel and I'd recognized him when I sat down. His photograph, marked with the key-letter for Totally Reliable, had been in the memorandum. Pol had said: "There are two people you can trust. An American, Frank Brand, and a young German, Lanz Hengel."

Before I'd recognized him I'd thought he was one of the adverse party, and that Phönix—if that was how they still styled their group—had set him to watch contacts of the Lindt girl. It would have tied in.

"Yes," I said, "he was a damned good man. But he was using cover and it didn't save him."

He said with a seething anger: "I was his cover."

"I know. Don't fret. That day in Dallas there were sixty Federal agents manning the inner ring."

"I was specially picked." He wasn't interested in Dallas.

"Then you're slipping." I'd had enough self-pity from the Lindt girl. "Five minutes' tag and I flushed you."

Polsknika "A": 775. Plus 5.
Portuguese Canning: 389. Plus 2¼.
Py-Sulpha: 452. Minus 10.

Coming up.

I'd asked Hengel: "Whose orders, to cover me?"

"I had no orders."

At least he was honest. "What's your current term in this field?"

"Two years."

He volunteered nothing, but just sat spiritually biting his lip. He had a good face but there was no guile in him. He lacked the element most necessary to his work: slyness. I wondered why they'd picked him to cover KLJ.

"You'll find plenty of games to play in two years, Hengel, but don't play any on my pitch. I told Pol no cover. It was called off as from last midnight."

If he had put up any argument I would have embarrassed him with a few facts. Where had he picked me up? He would know the address of my hotel but he hadn't picked me up from there or I would have sensed him. He couldn't have known I was going to the Neustadthalle because it was a last-minute decision: until I had Bourse clearance on Pol's photograph I wouldn't do anything active, so the Neustadthalle was a good passive search area for spending the day. He hadn't picked me up there, because I would have sensed him, and anyway he would have talked now about the crush attempt, especially as he was so desperate to cover me in the hope of saving my life and atone for the loss of KLJ. He'd never seen the crush attempt. He couldn't have known I went to the Lindt girl's flat or that I could be picked up from there when I left. There was only one answer: he'd seen me, by chance, about halfway along the Unter den Eichen, or one of the staff had seen me and told him and he'd started out on his own initiative. Local Control Berlin has two rooms, each with two windows, on the ninth floor of the corner building at Unter den Eichen and Rhönerallee, with front access through the passage at the side of the hat shop. The view of both streets is excellent and a lookout is normally stationed to make sure that any staff coming in has not been tagged to base by an adverse party. The lookout has a pair of Zeiss close-focus square-15's and can see the hairs on a fly at fifty yards. As one of the only three agents operating (in my case technically) from this base, I couldn't go down either of these streets without being seen. It had been halfway down the den Eichen that I had sensed the tag.

Hengel hadn't only lost me within five minutes but had picked me up by sheer chance, and he knew it. If I told him that I knew it too, he'd draw blood from his lip. If I told him he'd missed by ninety minutes an attempt on the life he was so eager to safeguard, he'd bust a gut.

So I just finished my beer and left him.

Back at the hotel I had some food and went up to tune in to Eurosound. The Bourse was being read now. My signal was just coming up.

Quota Freight Tenders: 878⅛. Plus 2⅛.
Rhone Electric: 626—

I switched off.

The "Communication Post and Bourse" system is limited but foolproof. One of our cipher staff dreamed it up himself. It is relatively safe to entrust a signal to the ordinary postal services, and in the Federal Republic as safe as anywhere in the world. The agent doesn't stamp his letters because it might not be easy at any given moment (when leaving a theater, for instance) to find a stamp. More important, an unstamped letter is virtually registered, since it must be handed personally to the addressee by the postman in order to collect the fee and tax. Thus, even if an agent is carrying a vital document and suspects he is being followed by an adverse party who might intend capturing the document at gunpoint at the first chance, he can get rid of it readily at the nearest post-box and insure its safety. We have a man at Eurosound to collect. Radio Eurosound is a perfectly genuine broadcasting station operating under the combined auspices of NATO and the Benelux Industrial Commune, and carries light music, U.S., British and French newscasts, and commercial programs.

The Bureau has facilities—not known publicly to exist—for inserting into the twice-daily Bourse price announcements the name and movement of a fictitious stock, in my case Quota Freight Tenders. (At the time of the Zossen operation, "Quota" was simply the call-sign—the memorandum being Q—and it could be varied five ways: Quota Freight Tenders in full, Quota Freight, Quota Tenders, Quota alone, and Q.F.T.) Each variation is in itself the keyword to one of four code systems, and the agent normally uses the book, because the permutations of a single "price" and "movement" (878⅛ plus 2⅛, in my case on that particular day) run into thousands of signals: the meaning of an 8 standing alone is different from that of an 8 appearing before a 7, and different again from that of an 8 before 78. Also, the fractions can change the whole of the signal given by the main digits. The "movement" of the share can in its turn change the signal formed by the "price." I possess no code book because a *systematic* permutation scheme can be committed to memory more easily than any random list of figures.

The Eurosound programs are legitimately aimed at an audience demanding light music for housewives, up-to-the-minute news flashes, and entertainment sponsored by the top Continental industrial concerns. That kind of audience does not want market news, and it would have been discontinued after the first probes by listener-research, but the sponsors insisted on two daily readings of the Bourse because their stock was listed and it gave them free publicity, especially when prices rose. The fact remains that since the inception of the Communication Post and Bourse system, no listener has ever telephoned Eurosound to ask who the hell Quota Freight Tenders *is* and where the stock can be bought.

The reply system has two advantages for an operator, especially when he must not carry radio. A letter mailed to him in reply to his would take longer and could be intercepted even if unstamped. A letter delivered to me at the Prinz Johann Hotel would have its tax paid by the desk and would be lying in a pigeonhole for as long as I was absent—sometimes a matter of days. Not safe. Nor is it convenient to pick up mail *Poste restante*; post offices are scarcer than beerhouses, and an agent would in any case have to carry the letter until he could burn it. He could be forced to give it up at gunpoint if an adverse party meant to have it. The second advantage of the P. and B. system is that it can reach an agent anywhere in Europe at a precise time when he can arrange to be alone to take the signal. Also, the signal goes *direct into his mind without trace.* He can, if he must, receive a signal while standing in a public bar with an adverse party at his elbow, and receive it in total secrecy. But it's a slow system and is never used in emergency. Emergency justifies risk, and the risk in any country is that the Bureau may, for many reasons, be working against the interests of that country's police services. In my case, a telephone call to Local Berlin Control would assume a risk and therefore be made only in emergency, because I was working against the interests of *certain members* of the Federal police services, the unknown ex- and neo-Nazis riddling the department from the highest echelons (people like Ewald Peters, just arrested) down to the constabulary. Any member of the police, seeing me leaving a telephone, could use his credentials and ask the hotel clerk, the barman, or the operator what number I had called, and could find the address. Also, the line could be tapped.

Against this risk we have two safeguards. There is a simple code system whereby "I'm dining with Davis tonight" means "I'm going to ground," and so on. If the signal is more complicated and a great deal of vital information has to be phoned in during an emergency, we speak in Rabinda-Tanath, the dialect of the Lahsritsa hill tribes of East Pakistan, which is even more basic than original Malay and has the advantage of being instantly adaptable. (Oddly, there is no word for "bullet," and we would use "kill-ball." "Motor-car" would be "fire-cart.") A Lahsritsa is stationed permanently in Local Control Berlin, happily studying for a degree in English literature between emergency calls.

There had been no urgency in getting confirmation of Pol's identity and function, so I had posted his photograph and set the system going. A photograph is always carried by an agent ordered to make contact with someone who has never met him before. Its receipt at the Bureau, without any message alongside, is taken to mean one thing: *Who is he?*

He was 878⅛. Plus 2⅛. *True name given. Totally reliable. Liaison London.*

That was why I'd never heard of him before. I'd been out of London for two years: Egypt, Cuba, now Germany. He was one of the new links normally liaising direct with London. I would never have seen him at all if KLJ hadn't bought it and thus created an emergency. Willi Pol (his Christian name had been in the memorandum) had been flown out to make contact and hand me the baby. Where was he now? Flying back. Lucky bastard.

Something about the darkened radio dial afflicted me, on the very edge of consciousness, and I worried it until the answer came. KLJ Petroleum had been knocked out of the market and wouldn't be quoted again.

I woke naturally at the top of a late sleep-curve and thought at once of her lean shoulders and the way she stood, because she'd been the last image of consciousness, quite unbidden.

There'd been a black panther in a dream, already fading. I beat around but couldn't bring it any clearer. It was too late. Dreams are gone in the first few seconds of waking, like ghosts at cockcrow. But she'd been there all right, a dark *succuba*.

Progress had been made in more practical directions. Before sleep I'd fed in the problem and by morning it was resolved. Decision: action this day.

I had assumed too much, and it had put me into a false position. I had assumed that the car had been out to crush me, and not the Lindt girl. I had assumed that the man who had begun tagging me along the Unter den Eichen was an adverse party: and I'd been wrong. I could have been wrong about the crush attempt too. They might not have been after me at all. They might not even know of my existence. My position would be false if I went on believing *necessarily* that while I hunted Zossen he hunted me.

So I still had to draw his fire. If they were already on to me, they'd stick, so I couldn't lose by taking action. I had to get where they wanted me, and hope to survive long enough for the overkill.

I was at the West Berlin Public Prosecutor's office before ten o'clock with a file on three suspects and a different set of papers showing me to be working in liaison with the Z Commission—which indeed I was. For six months I'd operated in strict hush; now I would head across open ground so that Phönix could see me.

"We knew nothing about these three people," Herr Ebert said plaintively.

"You do now, Herr Generalstaatsanwalt."

He nodded ponderously; his head was like a great smooth stone balanced upon another. I had checked his dossier months ago because I'd been working through his office indirectly, unknown to him, merely sending in the evidence as I gathered it and leaving him to pass on the orders of arrest to the Z Polizei. He was a Socialist and a Resistance veteran with a record of escapes from concentration camps equaled by few. The political cartoonist Federmann had pictured him with his huge arms carrying a Jewish child through the mud of littered swastikas, and the original sketch was framed on the wall above him. Invoking enemies by the hundred as he applied himself to ridding the German cupboards of their skeletons, he wished it to be known that of all the officials firmly astride the fence with a foot dabbling nervously on each side, he was not one.

I waited for twenty minutes while he rocked heavily in his chair reading my files. The evidence against these three men had been gathered during the last week, and I'd meant to hand it over to my successor to give him a good start. Now I would use it myself.

"This is very detailed, Herr Quiller."

"Yes."

"Your sources are obviously authentic. You must have worked very hard." He gazed at me from beneath pink-and-blond eyebrows. He wanted to know how I'd dug up all this without his ever having heard of me.

"You set a good example, Herr Generalstaatsanwalt."

His face remained bland. He let it go. Neither of us had time to play poker. "These are cases for immediate arrest."

"Yes."

"You'll perhaps give me the addresses where these men can be found."

"If you'll signal the Z Polizei, I'll go with them."

"That isn't necessary."

"No."

"But you wish to be in at the kill."

"Put it that way."

"I will arrange it." He lifted a phone.

It's always rather cozy when you are forced to do something you want to do but shouldn't. I shouldn't have allowed myself to be present at the coming arrests, because it was an indulgence; it would be a sadistic pleasure to watch the faces of these three men in their moment of nemesis, because I had last seen one of them—Rauschnig—inspecting a parade of young Jewish girls sent to him for "special treatment" at Dachau. They had been lined up naked against the wall of a corridor and he had selected ten of them for medical experimentation. I didn't know what had happened to them but I knew that their deaths wouldn't have been easy.

I had never met the other two—Foegl and Schrader—but from the evidence in the file they had excelled Dr. Rauschnig in acts of inhumanity. Therefore I would take pleasure in seeing their faces on this, the last day of their freedom.

This corrosive emotion would be out of place in the pursuit of an intellectual exercise; it wouldn't do me or anyone any good; but it would be incidental to my main purpose in going along with the Z Polizei. By the time the third arrest had been made, at my instigation and in my presence, Phönix would be on my track. That was the end of the means.

"A car will collect you in fifteen minutes, Herr Quiller." He gave me a signature for the receipt of the files. "Perhaps I shall have the pleasure of seeing you here again?"

"All going well, Herr Generalstaatsanwalt, I guarantee it."

The *Schönheitssalon* was in the Marienfelderplatz, and the three of us went through the doors together. The police captain and his sergeant were both armed but in civilian clothes. A screen of wrought filigree work intertwined with climbing flowers divided the little individual cubicles from the waiting-room. We were invited to sit but remained standing. A fountain played in a pink marble basin the shape of a shell and there were tiny tropical fish gliding in it. Pink gossamer curtains draped the walls and the lighting was shed from the centers of gilt sunbursts in the ceiling. The air was perfumed. A slender Venus stood in a softly illuminated niche, girdled with the gold riband of the Herr Direktor's diploma from the 1964 Exposition de Paris des Arts Esthètiques.

The receptionist came back: a heavy-bodied young *Mädchen* with jungle eyes. The Herr Direktor must oblige us to await him a further half hour, since he was in the middle of a delicate treatment and (the eyes dilated) the client was a baroness. The hem of her pink Grecian tunic swung as she turned away.

The police captain knew better than to trump this by presenting his credentials. The place would have more than one exit. I followed him with the sergeant through the low gilded gate.

Dr. Rauschnig was in the first cubicle. His face was plumper than when I'd last seen it, but I recognized him and nodded to the captain.

"Your name is Julius Rauschnig?"

Shocked at the intrusion, he declared his name to be Dr. Liebenfels. He had never heard of Rauschnig. The captain produced a photograph taken of Rauschnig in 1945 in the U.S. Army liberation sector, Dutch frontier. The photograph had been nameless-on-file in the Z Commission archives and I had picked it out for them this morning before coming here.

The woman on the treatment-couch bent her neck and peered at us with two affronted eyes in a half-applied mud pack. Then I turned my back because I didn't want to look any more at the face of Rauschnig. Corrosive emotions: no go.

His voice was bad enough to listen to. The harder it pretended indignation, the more it shook.

"I assure you that you are mistaken!" So on. "It is very harmful to the delicate facial tissues of the Baroness if the treatment is interrupted!" So forth. But I caught sight of one of his hands as it gesticulated, and the corrosion set in. Because a face is not active: it is only the shape of a name. It is the hand that acts. And these soft white hands that had been tenderly ministering to this woman's vanity, touching her withered face as if it were a flower in pretense that he could restore the bloom of youth, had once been laid upon the faces and the bodies of girls in Dachau as urgently as a beast claws meat.

His soft hands flew in the perfumed air. His voice bubbled in denial, more shrilly now. The woman, alarmed, called out, and the *Mädchen* in the Grecian tunic came trotting, to stand confused.

"You will please accompany me," the captain told him.

"I must telephone my lawyer!"

"We will telephone him from the gendarmerie."

"But I have no shoes for the snow! My chauffeur is not here with the car!"

"We have a car waiting."

"You cannot just take me like this from my work! This lady—"

"Herr Rauschnig, if you'll come with me peaceably there will be no inconvenience for anyone."

He began blubbering now and I concentrated on the young receptionist's face to take my mind from the sound; but her face was horrified and the light of the lamp was reflected in her eyes; and I'd noticed the lamp before I had turned my back. It had a small pink shade and I remembered the white shade of the lamp that had been in Hauptsturmführer Rauschnig's private quarters at the camp. The white shade, and a pair of gloves, and a book cover had been made by the deft fingers of his mistress who lived with him; by grace of a technique he had perfected, they were made of human skin.

"You cannot take me like this!" And the woman screamed as he

lurched past the girl. The sergeant tripped him automatically and he grabbed at the pink curtain, his shoulder smashing the thin partition of the cubicle as he fell and lay awkwardly, swathed in gossamer. The jar of mud pack *mousse* toppled from the treatment-table and spattered his legs. He lay babbling. I stepped over him and went out through the waiting-room and into the street and the sudden burst of a flashbulb.

"Wait," I told them. "They're bringing him out." I'd phoned Federal Associated Press from the offices of the Z Polizei, tipping them off.

When Rauschnig was led out, I moved to stand beside him as the flashes came again. By this evening my picture would be in several papers where Phönix could see it.

7 | RED SECTOR

The bullet from a small 8 mm. short-trigger Pelmann and Rosenthal Mark IV spins in the region of two thousand revolutions per second, and at very close range the flesh laceration is severe, due to heavy scoring by the large number of lands in the rifling. Carbon monoxide discharge is high and the flesh tattooing is consequently vivid. The bullet enters the body with the effects of an ultra-high-speed drill combined with a blowlamp.

In the case of Schrader, the skull had shattered badly and only one side of his face was recognizable. The police captain compared it with the profile photograph, took a statement from the secretary in the outer office, and then telephoned the *Selbstmord* department at Kriminalpolizei H.Q., since a suicide was more their job than his. Schrader would never go to trial and our interest in him was at an end.

I asked to be present at the summary search for papers and diaries but we turned up nothing that would lead me to Zossen. A phone call had been made not long before the shot was heard, from a man whose voice and name were unknown to the secretary. It was an hour since we had handed over Rauschnig and started out for Schrader, so someone must have sprung a big leak about Rauschnig's arrest and Schrader had decided not to face the music. It was because of this sort of thing that the Z Polizei liked to be quick when they could.

The captain was again annoyed to find the two energetic Federal Associated Press cameramen on the pavement outside the offices of Schrader-Fahben Shipping Components, and I didn't tell him I'd telephoned. It was usually relatives or friends who tipped off the next along the line when the Z went in and made a snatch, and the whole staff of the F.A.P. could buzz with news that wouldn't reach the close associates of arrested men until they printed it.

I made sure they got my picture and then went to find the car. It was a gray Volkswagen hired from Hertz on my sudden decision that morning: I wasn't a free agent, stuck in the back of the police car all the time, and it irked me. The VW was ubiquitous in shape and color and would make a useful mobile base if I had to stay away from the Hotel Prinz Johann for more than a day.

The black Mercedes followed me out of the city and through the snowscape. The sky at noon was dark against the white hills. The *Autobahn* through the Corridor was treacherous with stretches of black ice where last night the snow had turned to rain and the rain had frozen. There were few other cars on the route, and we were held up less than fifteen minutes at the Helmstedt checkpoint. I showed my second set of papers to avoid delay.

The Star of David School stood in a hollow of the land a few kilometers before Duisbäch. The snow on the courtyard was churned by children's feet, and they had built a snowman right in the center, with three faces so that he looked everywhere at once; two were nonsmokers and one had a pipe.

There was singing on the sharp air as we left the cars and made for the doors. The porch was stacked with galoshes and gum boots. The singing floated out across the soft white land, so that it seemed Christmas.

It was agreed that to avoid any scene that might worry the children, I should locate Professor Foegl alone and get him into the superintendent's quarters before Captain Stettner made the charge. The only person in view was a boy standing glumly outside a classroom in some kind of penance; he was cheered by the apparition of a stranger ignorant of his sins, and told me that Professor Foegl was in the hall where the singing came from. I went in quietly and stood for a while below the rostrum. The choir went a bit ragged and then forgot me, steadying. I watched the children and the man on the rostrum. His head was narrow and the face long and gentle; he closed his eyes now and then and his hands sketched slow rhythms in the air for the singers to follow; they sang almost faultlessly now, the full sweetness of their song drawn from them by the mesmeric hands; they sang as if they loved him.

When the canticle was ended, I clapped for the children and caused a total and embarrassed silence. I am no good with children, though I'd meant well. Forced to speak in a whisper, I told Professor Foegl that I was the representative of a music publisher and the superintendent would be glad if he could spare a few minutes in his office.

He said he would come. His voice was as gentle as his face. Only the eyes revealed the weakness that had brought him to this day; they were the eyes of a man who is ready to show fear, even when he is smiling.

We found the superintendent with the captain and sergeant. He'd obviously been primed; his face was set in the aftermath of shock. It was quiet in the room. We could hear one another breathing. The captain went into his routine and I saw the fear come flooding into the older man's eyes, and looked away.

"I must therefore ask you to come with me, Herr Professor."

"Yes," he said softly. His gentle head was raised and he stared through the windows at the black trees that stood in the snow, a group of waiting skeletons. "Yes," he said in soft answer to the summons he had lived in fear of, for twenty years.

They took him away. The superintendent had asked me to stay a moment.

"It's unbelievable," he said.

"I'm sorry."

"He was of my race." He stood staring at me and his hands were fumbling one against the other as if they were something he'd picked up and didn't know where to put. "Why did he betray us?"

"Out of fear."

"Was he tortured?"

"Not at that time. He knew he would have been if he refused to talk." For his sake I said: "It may be accepted in mitigation by the court."

"Mitigation?" I might have used a totally foreign word. "But there were thousands who were threatened with duress, and they didn't . . ."

"Hundreds of thousands. Millions. Six millions. He wasn't one of them. I'm sorry."

The *Blockwarts* had used him, and then the *Zellenleiters*, and the *Kreisleiters*, and at last the *Gauleiters*, playing on his fear and using him as a more and more valuable tool. The evidence on file recorded that he had *"caused the deprivation and ultimate death of his friends, his neighbors, and hundreds of his own kind, by revealing their names and hiding-places to the Gestapo."* The shortest and most graphic of the testimonies held him responsible for *"a good ten truckloads of deportees who had gone up the Auschwitz chimney."*

"Do you know anything about the Star of David School, Herr Quiller?" He was eying me reflectively, as if deciding to give me a confidence.

"It's modern, progressive, with a bias toward the Arts—"

"I don't mean that. Come to the window. I will tell you."

Beyond the window bay, the land rose gently toward the south. Behind the trees were scattered the black oblongs of roofs in the snow. There was the track of a stream running east-west through the floor of the hollow, but there were no willows to mark its banks.

"The school is modern and progressive, yes, and the Arts have a greater place in our curriculum than usual; but it has this in common with other schools: it's full of children. It was built for them especially. They run across these fields and climb those trees in freedom. It is their land, all theirs. And do you find the building it-self bright and well lighted with the big windows? And the décor vital with gay colors?"

I said I did.

"The architect was Joseph Steiner himself. Long rooms, wide corridors, a beautiful synagogue of white and purple stone from Bavaria, after the Finnish style of church. The children are very happy here. You can tell from their singing. You have heard them singing. You should see them in summer—that field is a carpet of clover and they picnic there. You should hear them sing on a sum-mer evening, Herr Quiller." He pointed through the window. "That looks like a stream, but it's really the remains of a railway embankment—a siding. The rails were taken up and used in the construction of the building, and the embankment has slowly fallen almost level with the meadow. The trucks used to come in there from Magdeburg, and that farm behind the trees was the medical experimentation block. The gas chambers were this side of the railway, here where we are standing. The foundations are built of their rubble. Some of the arrivals were hanged from those trees so that those who were brought here could see them and be warned about disobedience."

He turned from the window. "Few have heard of the camp, be-cause it was one of those successfully destroyed by the Nazis un-der the last-minute "Cloud Fire" order designed to obliterate evidence of atrocities. You won't find any record of it. But some knew of it." He turned his eyes on mine and I knew he wasn't look-ing at me but at men who had been here before me. "So we built this monument to our dead. We thought it was better than just a stone with a plaque. Some of the children laugh and play where their grandparents died. Of course they don't know it. This is in confidence, and I think you are a man to respect such a confidence. I have told you this because I can't believe this thing about Profes-sor Foegl. He was so gentle. The children are going to miss him, you know."

He suddenly flung out his hands. "But what made him come

here, to *us?* Did he know what this place used to be? Do you believe he knew?"

"He may have."

"Then why?"

"Remorse. Guilt. Cowards have the biggest consciences." I remembered how Foegl had stared out at those trees just now when he knew it was all up with him. "We don't know how much he might have been punishing himself, making himself face his past, everywhere he looked. It might have been that."

He stood for nearly a minute, motionless. Then he said: "I'm glad he's gone. This is holy ground." He suddenly offered his hand. "You'll have to forgive me. The choir had only just started, you know. I must go and do my best with them, but goodness knows I'm practically tone-deaf."

I walked through the wide glass doorway alone, between the rows of galoshes and gum boots. The tracks of the black Mercedes were on the snow. I looked across to the dark gnarled trees. For a minute the silence brooded, and I made myself wait, my breath half-held, standing beside the car.

Then it came again, the singing.

A thaw had set in and the evening streets were slushy. Snow was melting on the ruined shell of the Kaiser-Wilhelm Gedächtniskirche and the wrecked bones of its spire stuck into the sky, naked again and oddly beautiful.

Die Leute had me on the front page, a good full-face picture standing beside Rauschnig outside his beauty salon. Three other papers had the same picture, and two of them carried the later shot of the police captain and myself leaving the offices of Schrader-Fahben.

Other front-page news was that Franz Röhm, Secretary of the Road Safety Committee, had hanged himself, as I had known he would.

It would have been difficult to get photographers down to the

Star of David School because we didn't want the children worried, but I had sent in the word to F.A.P., and *Die Leute* carried a picture of Professor Foegl and a full paragraph, linking him with Rauschnig and Schrader and commenting on the "lightning wave of arrests" that marked the day. I would therefore be linked, myself, with the Foegl snatch, and Phönix wouldn't miss it.

They gave me half an hour with Foegl in his cell but I was out of luck. His fear—which I'd hoped would be the mainspring of ready confession—had gone, after twenty years. The worst had come to him and he knew his life would end in a cell like this, so he had nothing more to fear. I doubted if even the fullest confession would count for an acquittal, but I tried the idea on him. He wouldn't budge. He seemed to have already faded away in a kind of death.

They had a lock-up for the Hertz VW at the Hotel Prinz Johann, and I backed it in. Slush dripped from the wings and a puddle of water had formed on the concrete before I left it and went in to a late meal. Some of the staff stared at me a bit because they'd seen the papers, and the wine steward had a grayness about his face. He was past middle age, and as his slightly shaking hand poured my wine I wondered where he'd been between '39 and '45, and what he'd done.

But the wine's flavor was unspoiled. After six months on a dung heap you don't notice the smell.

Most of the tables had been cleared by the time I was served with the coffee. The American drew a chair near and dropped his evening paper onto the table. I glanced down at my own face and up into his. He said with a pleasant smile:

"Seems we're sailing a little close to the wind, sir."

I didn't want to talk or even know him but there is sometimes a danger in not responding and the strict orders are to do so, at once.

"Catch it as it comes, and the closer the better."

So this would be Brand. A flat shrewd face with level gray eyes and a crew cut. The smile was pleasant, but I resented him and resented his cheeking me. If an agent decides to splash his pan all over the front page there is obviously a reason, and it's his own business. He goes to work his own way, on one condition: that he doesn't endanger secrecy. It had to be accepted that if I decided to draw enemy fire the only one to get hurt was me. Now that my face was being advertised, I couldn't go within a mile of the Unter den Eichen and Rhönerallee intersection even if I were certain there was no tag. In starting out to expose myself to the adverse party deliberately, I had implicitly cut myself off from Local Control except for Post and Bourse, the sole safe line of communication. I'd become, since this morning, a "hot operator," whom no one wanted to go near. It was a classic move, and KLJ had used it twice in his career, breaking the normal conditions of strict hush and meeting the enemy on open ground as the most expedient way of doing a particular job. It is dangerous for the agent and he knows it and settles for it. It is more dangerous for him if people don't keep clear of him, and it becomes dangerous for them. A hot operator must have no cover, no contacts, and must never go near Control. Even a radio is dangerous.

"How long are you staying?" I asked him uncivilly.

"Oh, I practically live here."

We both knew that in a place like this we had to converse cautiously, so that even if a tape-recording were made it wouldn't give anything away. There were columns and curtains in this room, and waiters were still on the move. The table could even be miked.

He offered me a small cigar but I shook my head. "I don't know this brand."

"I just thought I'd introduce it to you." He put the cigar wallet away.

"I'm hot," I said, looking at the windows. He picked up his paper.

"You kid me not." He grinned quickly, glancing at the front-page picture. He tucked the paper under his arm. "Well, I'll leave you in peace. Always at your disposal, of course."

I watched him away, took ten minutes to finish my coffee, and went up to my room, changing into dry shoes and mentally listing all the good reasons against what I was going to do. Then I switched on to light music, a few minutes before time.

I used the hotel paper.

Repeat: There is to be no cover. Hengel made contact. I don't like this. Brand has made contact and is staying here. I don't like this either. Repeat: am operating solo.

The music stopped.

I decided, through the first half of the report, not to finish the note yet.

Portuguese Canning: 388. Minus 1.
Py-Sulpha: 459. Plus 7.
Quota Freight: 793⅝. Plus 10⅝.
Rhone Electric: 625—

I switched off. It read: *All precautions. Yourself red sector.*
I finished the note.

If no confidence in my policy you have only to say so, and pull me out. Q.

People were making me too angry and that was bad because emotions clutter up clear thinking on a job. I'd let the Hengel boy off lightly, saying only that he'd made contact and not saying that he'd picked me up on his own initiative and then let me flush him within minutes. I didn't want Control to rap him, only to keep him out of my way. But it had made me angry. So had Brand, contacting me when he knew damned well I was a hot operator. Even if Control hadn't warned him, he should have known as soon as he saw my picture on the front page linked with a "lightning wave of arrests." Now Control itself had made me angry. "All precautions"—in other words, I wasn't to risk endangering secrecy by these wildcat methods I was embarked on. "Yourself red sector"—I was exposing myself to enemy fire.

Did I need telling?

Let them call my bluff and try to pull me out. They wouldn't succeed. I was out for Zossen. They'd given a dog a bone.

I took the VW as far as the Wilmersdorf district and posted the signal, locking the car and walking the rest of the way to her flat, angry, finally, with myself, because of all the good reasons I had mentally listed against going there again.

8 | INGA

Within twenty-four hours they had me. During
this period there were small signs of their closing in, and I was
content to wait for them.

It was midnight when I got back to the hotel from Inga's flat.
She'd been on edge and had tried not to show it. The dog had been
sent to bed: it had a kennel on the roof and went up by the fire escape. She'd said, "Friend," and it went off without another look at
me. Mostly we'd sat drinking and listening to things like "Night
Bounce" that she put on the record-player for me, an eerie tune
that suited her personality, lean, brooding, and cynical. She wore
an all-black after-ski outfit more like a skin-tight track suit with the
top slit to the waist, and a thonged belt. Nudity would have been
less explicit.

I didn't alter my identity: I was still with the Red Cross tracing
relatives of refugees. She mentioned Phönix twice, during one of
her bitter reminiscences, and spoke once of Rothstein. I hooked
his name immediately because I hadn't known he was in Berlin. If
there were a chance, I would look him up.

Sometimes, watching her, I wondered: *What sex are you?* She
must have known that she was getting under my skin, by all the
things we didn't say. There was a rapport between us that made
long silences unembarrassing even when the music wasn't playing
and the room was totally silent. Tonight she smiled sometimes, and

not altogether cynically. Lean, black, leather-belted and athletic-looking, gold hair thick along her arms: she might be anything. Lesbian, narcissist, sado-masochist, necrophile, any or all, and nothing for me, which was why I was here, a nihilist.

She knew that I wondered about her, and teased me, using her body as she moved in the light and shadow cast by the Chinese-moon lamp, displaying its moods of poise, rhythm, tension, and repose, miming an animal and begetting images whose shapes we shared, hideous and comical according to caprice, so that I was at once repulsed and bespelled. She was a houri at the court of Thanatos, and had learned her darkness in the Führerbunker, just as I had learned mine among the legions of the damned. This was our touchstone and we both knew it.

When I left her we had not even kissed; we had done more and less than that. *Inga*. Her name rang in me.

The streets were deserted and the gutters arush with the thaw, and my trudging footsteps echoed among the buildings. A moon was out, scything the dark clouds. The colors of the neon signs ran melting over wet stones, and the Kreuzberg floated like a green island in the sky.

The Volkswagen was still where I'd left it in the Hohenzollern-platz, and I checked the door handles and keyslot with my bare fingers for nicks in their metal. The match I had rigged inside the driving-door hinge fell away. The car hadn't been touched.

I started up and headed south through Steglitz, checked the car behind, turned right, rechecked, turned right-left-right, re-checked, and added up the score. This was: it hadn't been touched but it had been watched. They'd tagged me from the Hotel Prinz Johann to Wilmersdorf and let me go, waiting for me to come back. Now they were tagging again. I claim always to know when I am being followed, on foot. Flushing a tag by car is more difficult, sometimes impossible, because the traffic conditions occupy too much of the attention. Tonight I knew they were there, within the first mile of leaving the Wilmersdorf area, because the streets were empty: but they'd followed me four hours ago from the hotel to

Wilmersdorf without my knowledge, because the traffic had been heavy.

She was a gun-metal-blue DKW F-102 *Viertürer* with the four distinctive Auto Union rings on the rad-slats.

This, then, was the first of the small signs that they were closing in on me. Closing in—no more than that. They weren't after a kill or I would have been dead by this time. I was working on the assumption that they were too intelligent to kill me out of hand simply because I'd done a snatch on Rauschnig, Schrader, and Foegl. Several hundred war criminals had been herded into a dozen Federal courts since the London Agreement had triggered the hunt, and no one working for the Z Commission had been shot at. It would have led to a minor war, and it seemed to be the present policy of Phönix to keep hush. Those lost souls—Schrader, Röhm, and a dozen others—who had taken a P. and R. Mark IV or kicked a chair from under them had been put under pressure by their own kind or had just got tired of waiting for the knock on the door. Those like Kenneth Lindsay Jones, who were killed off by the adverse party, were the subject of simple murder, but they weren't killed out of hand. They were vetted first. As far as the Bureau knew, KLJ hadn't been caught and grilled before they finished him off, but then a dead man can tell his Bureau precious little. He *may* have been caught and grilled before the kill: that would be their policy. Squeeze the lemon before you throw it away. Or, if he'd been smart enough to dodge them at every turn, they may have simply decided that he was getting too close for comfort and must be stopped.

But I was all right, Jack. They didn't even know I was going for Zossen. All they knew was that a strange face had suddenly turned up on the front page alongside Rauschnig's and that I'd been in on the Schrader death and the Foegl snatch. They knew the faces of the Z Polizei very well. They didn't know mine, and they wanted to. At the moment, they were watching it in a mirror at a hundred yards' range and they meant to get closer than that. More important, they wanted to know where I was going. They knew about the

ADAM HALL

hotel because they'd picked me up there, so they weren't just tagging me home.

We went right, left, right, and across the Innsbruckerplatz through drifts of slush. There was no point in trying to lose them because they knew where I lived, but after the brooding sex-and-*Götterdammerung* claustrophobia of Inga's flat, I felt like a bit of healthy schoolboy action and decided to give them a run. It would have to be quick because we were already hitting the limit and there'd be a police patrol mixing with us before long, and there mustn't be any publicity of that kind. One thing to get your face in a news photo, another thing to submit to police laws and show them all your papers. Mine were so well forged that even infra-red would reveal the same fibers, but I didn't want to have any personal details printed even in a back-page filler because it would involve the Red Cross. Nor has the Bureau any kind of diplomatic immunity from contravention of traffic regulations. It doesn't exist.

Slush was coming up onto the windscreen and the wipers knocked it away. We made a straight run through Steglitz and Südende because I wanted to know if they'd now make any attempt to close right up and ram. They didn't. They just wanted to know where I was going. I'd have to think of somewhere. Their side lamps were steady in the mirror, a pair of pale fireflies floating along the perspective of the streets. We crossed the Attilastrasse and I made a dive into Ringstrasse going southeast, then braked to bring them right behind me and make them slow. As soon as they had, I whipped through the gears and increased the gap to half a block before swinging sharp left into the Mariendorferdamm and heading northeast toward the Tempelhof. Then a series of dives through back streets that got them going in earnest. The speeds were high now and I had the advantage because I could go where I liked, whereas they had to think out my moves before I made them, and couldn't, because I didn't know them myself until the last second.

They lost me once and came up broadside-on by luck at the

north end of a block, and once they hit something in a slide and the sound echoed between the walls of the narrow street. They were getting worried, certain now that I must be heading for a destination that had to be kept secret.

The mount of the Kreuzberg was ahead of us, and I swerved right by *Flughafen* station and then backtracked because we were getting too close to the Hotel Prinz Johann and I wanted them to keep thinking I was going somewhere else, somewhere important, before I made an all-out effort to lose them and leave them guessing.

Their lights were close behind me at the Alt-Tempelhof and Tempelhoferdamm crossing, and then I saw them flick out. There was no tire-squeal because of the slush; there were only a few long seconds of comparative silence before the sound of the crash filled the buildings like an explosion. I was placed in a slow drift for a right-angle when I heard it, and brought the nose round full-lock with the curb for a cush. The impetus of the DKW had sent it back across the street in a ricochet, and I saw it hit a parked Opel broadside-on in a smother of slush and debris. Then it took fire.

My half-spin had brought me to a halt alongside the curb, so I doused the lights and sat there. A man was screaming. The doors of the car didn't come open. I think if I'd tried, I could have sprinted those thirty yards and got a door open and a man out before the flames took hold. I didn't try.

Because they were the enemy. In war, even in war, when death is the object of all human enterprise, there are small acts of chivalry when a man, being gentle in himself despite the orders to kill, performs a gentlemanly deed and redeems by a little the monstrous stupidity of his kind. But the soldier is not alone. He has the brotherhood in arms of a whole regiment behind him, and be they nowhere near at hand they are in his mind.

We are alone. We are committed to the tenets of individual combat and there is no help for him who falls. Save a life and we save a man who will later watch us through the crosshairs and squeeze the trigger if he gets the orders or the chance. It's no go. The car burned and the man screamed and I sat watching. We are not gentlemen.

That was the first of the small signs that we were in business. The second manifested itself not long after dawn the next morning. It was nearer home.

The light in the Schönerlinderstrasse was pale gray. Mist covered the airfield, rising from earth sodden from the thaw. There had been no aircraft movement for the last two hours: I had woken at half past five, and there had been silence from the Tempelhof. The beacon was still flashing, its rays becoming fainter on the ceiling as the daylight strengthened.

I'd been thinking about Inga, and realized it, and threw her out of my thoughts. The living mustn't haunt; the dead were quite enough.

But I would try to see Rothstein. She had mentioned him.

The air in the room was cold, like metal against the face. I shut the window, and saw the second small sign. It was a twin glint. The street was empty but for a cruising taxi, and I remembered I must take care today: they'd missed their target against that wall and might be waiting to do a better job for their vanity's sake. (*Had* it been meant for her, that time, or me? I still wasn't sure. Another thing: Phönix might be no better integrated than any other big organization, and the right hand in big organizations doesn't always know what the left hand's doing. Top orders were to keep me on ice, or I'd have been dead by now; but some thick-ear minion with a stolen taxi might be out for blood on his own account or even for revenge because of the man who'd screamed.)

The taxi turned the corner, and the street fell quiet again but for the bang of my window. The twin glint had been framed by a window opposite. It doesn't matter how far back you stand in a room; a stray reflection may sometimes be caught across the field-glass lens. It might have been the bright roof of the taxi. There is always something you can do about being followed: you can flush the tag once you have seen him. There is nothing you can do about being watched. You can draw the curtains but that won't help you when you go down the steps into the street.

I dressed, listening to the radio. The morning Bourse announcement gave only the call-sign: Q.F.T. and a gibberish of figures. There was a seven o'clock special delivery to Eurosound because they ran three quiz programs a week and an audience research team, and certain schedules were dependent on the mail. So our man would have just got my letter and they'd decided on a pained silence in answer to my bleat.

It took twenty minutes to locate Dr. Solomon Rothstein in the new-subscriber addendum of the directory. I hadn't meant to see him right away because I would be in Berlin another month; but it would be more difficult later when they closed in on me and we were at grips. I didn't want him harmed, after all that had gone before.

Then I went down the steps into the street.

It may have been subliminal fear that had kept me so long at the directory. The id, alarmed by the plans of the ego (to go down those steps), had put up defenses, tricking me into missing the name the first time and leading me into a series of delaying errors, hoping that we might call the whole thing off. No go. I had made up my mind to see Rothstein, and that meant the steps. The only other exits from the hotel were via the kitchens and the main fire escape. Neither could be used unless I was under fire.

There were seven steps. They had been swept free of the melted snow, and sand had been laid. It was gritty beneath my shoes. After the first two steps I was fully exposed to that window across the street, and my breath came short, involuntarily. It happens when you wade into cold water: it catches your breath but you wade on deeper and deeper because you know the feeling will pass. You know that it's only the cold.

They are only field glasses.

With luck. But look what happened to Kenneth Lindsay Jones. Five steps, six, seven. Too late now for them to do anything even if they wanted to, because I was moving at right angles along the pavement. They would have fired direct into me on the steps if they'd meant to. The street seemed achingly silent in contrast with what my ears had been listening to subconsciously: the shot.

I was annoyed with myself. There wasn't a president of any republic in the world who didn't have to walk through that kind of risk whenever he showed himself in the open. I was annoyed more by my admission of the fear than by the simple fact of its existence. It is always present, all the time; without it we should all die young. But I was thinking about it, consciously, and I didn't like that. Six months' hard in strict hush had left the nerves exposed.

There was sweat on me before I turned into the gates to the lock-ups, and I thought: *You poor bastard, you're getting old.*

The Volkswagen ran through flooded streets. Rothstein had a laboratory in the Zehlendorf district, on the top floor of a building in the Potsdamerstrasse. He was alone when I called, and for an instant he didn't recognize me. Then his eyes changed.

"Quill . . ." He took both my hands.

"Hello, Solly."

We'd met in Auschwitz and had seen each other only once since then, almost by chance, with no time to ask of our affairs. So this was the third meeting and I was always to remember it, because if I had not called on him that day he might have lived.

9 | THE KILL

"It was a long time," said Solly in English.

"Yes."

He didn't mean since our chance meeting in Munich three years ago, but since Auschwitz.

The day I first met him we got seventeen out and only four of them touched the high-voltage wire. The rest lived and were alive now, as far as I would ever know. Solly was one of them. He joined us afterward. At that time I had linked up with three men: a Berliner Jew, a Pole, and a Dane. Before linking with anyone, I had worked solo for three years and my bag was some ninety-seven souls. After linking and forming a team, we got more than two hundred out before the liberation of the south camps.

Most of that time I was working as a low-intelligence pure Aryan camp guard, ex-seaman, with an uncle in Himmler's Einsatzgruppen hierarchy. I used to curse Churchill with such versatility that they made me do it on the stage once as part of the act when they ran a variety show the night before the gas chambers were ceremonially opened. I went over big. We got seven out that same night, because we'd been told that the capacity of the new gas chambers was estimated at two thousand per day and the camp commandant got drunk to celebrate, and most of his officers got drunk too. We didn't. Seven out of two thousand seemed so little.

Solly and I went back to Auschwitz after it was over, and showed the Allied troops where we'd cemented over a hole in the wall of the punishment-block to conceal the records we'd been making for three or four months. The evidence hanged nine S.S. officers and fourteen guards, but we didn't have a drink on that either; all the time we were collecting the evidence it had seemed important, but later we saw it wasn't. It had simply helped to keep our spirits going, to scratch the face of Satan.

Solly hadn't changed much in twenty years. His face had changed—we'd been young men then—but his spirit was still the same. You would call him the gentlest of men, and so he was, unless made angry. He was possessed of an anger that didn't show; it was as calm as the undetonated elements of a bomb.

I could sense the dormant anger in him now, and knew that he would never be at peace.

"I heard last night that you were in Berlin," I said.

"And you come to see me at once. How good that is of you!"

You can go through the fires of hell itself with a man and have nothing to say when you meet him again, unless it's "And do you remember old So-and-so?" There was no one we wanted to remember.

"What are you doing in Berlin?" he asked me, and we talked like that for a while. We were alone in his office, but we could see the heads of two men, his assistants working in the laboratory. The partition had a glass panel.

"Is it still bugs, Solly?"

"Oh, yes!" He smiled, for he had a thousand million children whom he loved. When we had chanced to meet, in Munich, he was a member of the international convention of bacteriologists who were gathered there to discuss some proposal or other about germ warfare. It wasn't in my line, but he was an accepted authority. "The University of Cologne gives me a grant of money," he said, "so I have my own laboratory!"

"Congratulations. Frankly it gives me the creeps." There were control canisters crawling with molds and cultures all over his office. He talked about some of his work and interrupted himself often, gazing at me in a kind of hellish rapture. More than once he cocked his head up and peered through the glass partition and then turned to me as if he were on the brink of some vital confidence. Then his eyes dulled and I could see the control he had clamped down on his impulse to confide. It was then that he looked as I had seen him when they had separated the men from the women as they were driven down the ramps from the trucks. When they had dragged his young wife from him he had stood like this, his eyes dull in a kind of passing death.

After a time he stopped telling me about his work, and there was nothing else to say and we knew it.

"Where are you staying?" he asked me. "We must meet again!" I told him and he said: "The Prinz Johann? That is expensive!"

"I never sleep in cheap hotels in Germany." I don't know why I said it: just a thought-flash. At Ravensbrück they had always cut the hair from the women before gassing them, and the hair was steamed and baled for transport to the mattress factories. The best hotels in Germany have foam rubber.

"We will meet again, then!" he said when he saw that I wanted to go. I said yes, we certainly would; but we didn't make a date.

Back in the street I wished I'd never called on Solly Rothstein. Did he, up there with his bugs, wish I had never called? I'd left him frustrated: there had been something vital he'd been burning to tell me, and couldn't. There was the feeling in me that I wouldn't want to know.

He phoned me in the late afternoon. I shall always remember my carelessness.

He said in English: "It is me."

I didn't answer. For some reason I was thinking about Pol. Then Solly said: "It was a long time, wasn't it?"

"Yes." He had wanted to identify himself without giving his name.

"I will come to see you," he said. "Wait for me."

The line went dead.

So he couldn't keep it to himself. The frustration was too much. Either that, or he'd been unwilling to tell me in the laboratory: the partition had been thin. He had decided, *after* I had left there, to talk to me; otherwise he would have made a date for a meal somewhere, on the spot. He didn't trust the phone: no names. He didn't trust the thin partition.

It wasn't only bugs, then. Or it was bugs in a big way. Germ warfare might be the clue. But I was still thinking of Pol, and about the box office of the Neukomödietheater, so I worried it. There must be a connection. Pol wouldn't phone me here; I was hot, untouchable, unphonable. His voice wasn't anything like Solly's, and Pol had spoken only German to me. Not the connection. Must be one. I had to recall actual conversation between Pol and me before I got it. He'd said:

We knew that you had reserved this box.

So you've got access to the box office.

Yes.

No go. I used the name Schultze.

We knew that.

By tapping my phone.

I bruised my hand hitting the receiver in a blind grab and caught it as it began falling. I knew the laboratory number because I'd hooked it automatically in the memory when I'd shut the directory. Switchboard told me to wait.

I waited. A nerve had begun flickering in my eyelid.

Carelessness. There had been a click on the line when I'd answered Solly's call. I hadn't expected a call from anyone, not from Pol, Hengel, Ebert, Inga, Brand, anyone I could think of. In no situation would Pol, Hengel, or Brand phone me here. Ebert didn't have my number; nor did Inga. Solly wouldn't phone me, because we hadn't even made a date to meet again. Then who? Consciously involved with the question, I'd heard the click on the line only subconsciously, and it had chain-reactioned in the memory so that I'd begun thinking of Pol and the box office, for no known reason.

My phone was being tapped again. Not by Control this time: that had just been a hush way of finding me. This time it was by the adverse party. The DKW tag. The twin glint. Now the tap. The third small sign that they were closing in.

"The number's ringing, sir."

"Thank you."

The eyelid went on flickering.

It didn't matter that they were tapping me now, at this minute, because all I had to tell Solly was *don't come!*

I might be wrong but couldn't chance it. Solly would trust neither a phone nor the partition in his own laboratory; therefore he was in some kind of permanent red sector and had to watch everything he did; therefore he might be known to Phönix, so well that they even knew his voice. He might be doubling with them, still feverish with that undetonated anger of his after twenty years, playing his own game with them in order to get facts that would guide him along the fuse to that almighty detonation he must have before he died, however long it took, because of his young wife.

"Dr. Rothstein's laboratory."

I said: "I'd like to speak to him."

"He's just left here, I'm afraid. Can I give him your message?"

"There's no message."

I put the receiver down.

Solly Rothstein was burning to tell me something and it was something so vital that no one must overhear. If they knew him, and knew his voice, they would know that he was on his way here now, because of the tap. And they would try to stop him. And there was nothing I could do.

The Zehlendorf district was ten kilometers from the east side of the Tempelhof, so he wouldn't walk all the way. Nor would he simply take his car or a taxi from door to door; his tactics were already cautious; he would dodge about. Hopeless to start out from here and try to intercept him. Must wait here for him.

Time-check: 5:09. Ten kilometers by car or taxi through the beginning of the rush hour: twenty minutes. Add five, because he'd start out on foot if he were taking a taxi and pick it up some distance from base; or he'd take it from base and leave it some distance from here. He might even take a trolley or the overhead, but it was unlikely because he was impatient. He would be here between twenty minutes and half an hour from now. 5:29 to 5:39.

I didn't phone the laboratory again to ask if he normally used a car or taxis because they would tap me, and if they'd no plans for Solly at this moment I didn't want to suggest they should make any. If I were wrong, nothing would happen. If I were right, they would be doing all they could to reach him along his route. A car would come into his mirror and stay there, waiting for the chance; or a man would open the door of his taxi and climb in while it was held at the lights; or someone would cross the road and fall in behind him along the pavement.

5:14. Nothing to do.

I left my room and went along the corridor until I found a door open. The room was empty. The curtains were filmy but opaque enough by winter daylight. Five minutes' gradual movement and the hem was parted an inch from the window frame, and I checked the apartments across the street. The window four up and seven along was open, a dark square. I let the curtain fall and came away.

At 5:23 I went down and wandered around the main reception lounge, keeping within sight of the switchboard so that the girl would recognize me and know I wasn't in my room, because Solly might conceivably phone again if he sensed he was being followed.

At 5:27 I went through the revolving doors and down the steps and crossed the road and stood well back in the doorway of the apartments, so that my head would have to turn only about a hundred and twenty degrees instead of one-eighty to keep each end of the street under alternate observation. He might come from either direction.

My breath floated gray on the cold air. Tires hissed along wet tarmac. Two men came down the steps of the Prinz Johann and turned west side by side. Time: 5:34. Didn't matter now, just have to wait and go on waiting. Cold. Cold outside and cold inside. Carelessness, bloody carelessness. Getting old.

A Borgward pulled in at the curb and I had to shift my position to keep the east end of the street under watch. Present population of street: woman and dog ten degrees left coming east, man black overcoat ninety degrees right coming west, two girls one-double-o right catching up, hear their voices, one laughing. Two men (same two?) extreme left coming east (coming back?). Borgward away, gas acrid on the air. Shift position. Girls passing black overcoat. Man extreme right coming west. Check left, check right. Walking quickly, short, black hat. Check left, check right. Yes.

I left the doorway and walked slowly at first to keep him under scrutiny and when the distance was fifty or sixty yards and I could recognize him with certainty, I quickened and took a gap in the traffic and crossed over. We were closing on each other from thirty yards and all I had in my pockets were keys but they'd have to do. Twenty yards and within calling distance. Stop. Check. Four up and seven along—and I was running, calling his name and shouting for him to dodge. He saw me, surprised. I flung the keys full at his face and they whistled through the air but never hit him because he was staggering, toppling, as the thin crack of sound echoed across the blank stone face of the buildings.

I caught him as he fell.

"Solly," I said to him, "it was my fault."

He didn't hear.

10 | THE NEEDLE

I phoned the Z Polizei within ten minutes and said:
"You may like to get some men along to 193 Potsdamerstrasse,
top floor, a laboratory. Make sure they're armed. I'm expecting
some trouble there."

I recognized the captain's voice. He said:
"We've just sent a squad in. There was a call from there not long
ago reporting a raid. Papers were taken."

"Get them back if you can. Listen, please: I have an address for
you. Concierge's office, main entrance, the Mariengarten building,
middle of the Schönerlinderstrasse, Tempelhof." He was repeating, so that a clerk could get it down. "The laboratory is run by Dr.
Solomon Rothstein. He's just been shot dead in the street outside
the Mariengarten building and I've brought him in here. Shot was
fired from a window of the Schönerpalast on the other side of the
street, fourth floor, seven windows from the east end of the block.
Telescopic rifle. Ambulance already laid on for Dr. Rothstein. I
shall be here when you come."

I left the porter in charge of the body and pushed through the
crowd in the entrance, going across to the Schönerpalast and hurrying the concierge into the lift, saying: "The Kriminalpolizei will
be here in a few minutes and no one must go into the room until
they arrive." He asked me what had happened and I just told him it

was a homicide case. "I want the seventh window from the end of this corridor."

It was room 303. The door pushed open easily and I didn't even bother to check the hinge-side gap for anyone standing behind it. The marksman would have been out of this room and this building before I had carried the body into the Mariengarten. There was nothing unusual about the room except that it was cold in contrast to the corridor. The concierge went to shut the window and I stopped him. "Don't touch anything, please." There was some grease-proof paper, empty, with the word LUNCHPAK printed on it, on the floor by the window. An ashtray was heaped with cigarette butts.

I looked down across the street. The ambulance was just pulling up. Two men cleared a way through the small crowd of people, one of them carrying a rolled stretcher. I told the concierge to lock the door of the room and wait for the police to come.

It was necessary for me to keep active and not think about Solly. That would come later; remorse—worse, guilt—would set in like a rot and I would never be wholly free of it. I had never counted the men I had killed during the last thirty years, nor had the thought of their dying ever concerned me. Most of them had been Nazis during the short period of the war; the rest had died because they were in the act of attempting to kill me. They had all been enemies. Solly had been a friend and I'd killed him by carelessness.

Before the setting-in of permanent remorse there would be this immediate phase of self-fury to combat, and action was the sole anodyne.

A black Mercedes was stationed behind the ambulance when I went down and crossed the road, but I turned left along the pavement and went into the yard of the hotel and got out the Volkswagen. I headed due west and reached the Potsdamerstrasse inside fifteen minutes by taking the new perimeter road round the airport and playing the lights on the amber most of the way.

The captain was still at the laboratory. He had followed up the emergency-squad after my call to him. He was the Z officer who'd been with me on the Rauschnig-Schrader-Foegl operation. His name was Stettner. He said:

"What happened to Dr. Rothstein?"

"Nothing more than I told you."

"We sent the homicide people along. Did they get your report?"

"No. They can have it later. I wanted to see this place."

The two laboratory assistants were there, looking shaken. The raid had been quick and not too thorough: some of the culture canisters had been knocked onto the floor and their glass was smashed. A sergeant was gathering the last of the research files for removal.

The pattern was clear enough. Phönix had known Solomon Rothstein. They had suspected him of doubling with them and had said nothing. Possibly they had found out that he had been working with me in the last months before the capitulation. Certainly they had tested him within these final twenty-four hours: I knew that. And they had not only tapped my phone; they had tapped his. Then, when they heard him say that he was coming to see me, they were certain, and they went into action. There had been no one close enough to his laboratory to catch him as he left, so they'd had to pass the orders to the man in room 303. If he hadn't already had the rifle they would have taken it to him. (But I think he already had the rifle because it might have been policy at any time to pass him an order to kill, with myself as the subject.) And even before he had reached the Schönerlinderstrasse they'd ordered the search of his laboratory, because they knew that I'd go there hoping to find out what vital thing it was that he hadn't been able to tell me.

I looked at the broken glass. Glass, broken, looks so irredeemable. It is one of the few things that we can never mend.

"Have you found anything?" I asked the captain. He was looking at me intently, and said:

"He was your friend?"

So I was showing it.

I said: "Yes. Have you found anything?"

"These files. A few other papers."

"Nothing special?" I knew he was balking me because his training had told him never to talk to strangers, even when they were sent to liaise with him by an intelligence directive.

He was still watching me. I stared him back. At last he said: "This."

It was an oblong box about fifteen by thirty centimeters, black-painted metal with two grimp seals. A strip of paper was secured along the top side with transparent tape.

In the event of my death, please send this container by airmail to my next-of-kin: Isaac Rothstein, 15 Calle de Flores, Las Ramblas, San Caterina, Argentina. To be opened by himself personally. S.R.

I said: "Are you going to mail it?"

"It won't be my decision, but I doubt it. We shall probably send for Isaac Rothstein to come and open it in our presence." He passed the container back to the sergeant. "We are leaving now, Herr Quiller. Do you want to make any inquiries of your own?"

"No. I'll read the report you're given by these two people when they've been fully questioned."

They drove to the Z Polizei bureau in their car; I followed in the VW. The traffic was heavy. Night had come, and the city was dining out to celebrate the thaw. I couldn't be certain there was no tag, but it wasn't important. They were closing right in on me now.

The homicide office had apparently put out a dragnet for me in the last hour, and I was asked to go over there and make my report on the shooting. It took ten minutes. They read it and kept me a full hour trying to probe my background. I kept strict hush. In the end I got bored and said:

"If you can't get enough clues out of room 303, try the Potsdamerstrasse laboratory. Try my own room at the Prinz Johann as well if you like—they'll have had the paper off the walls by now."

This appeared to interest them. "Are you returning there yourself?"

"Yes."

"Then we can send someone with you."

"Why not?"

Then the phone rang and he listened a minute and passed the receiver to me. It was Captain Stettner of the Z Polizei.

"Will you please come over, Herr Quiller?"

"I've just been there."

"This is very important."

I said I would go over. The homicide man was annoyed, because his bureau and the Z Polizei were out of gear with each other. Their fields overlapped and they were constantly thrown into each other's pitch. They thus looked for every chance of making the situation worse so that sooner or later some administrative top kick would be obliged to define their provinces more clearly. People like me were useful as a ball to lob about.

"You are not returning with us to the Hotel Prinz Johann, Herr Quiller?"

"No."

"But you have just said—"

"The phone call was urgent. I'm officially in liaison with the Z Commission. Simple as that, Herr Inspektor."

It was a ten-minute drive. I put the VW into the reserved parking area outside the Z Bureau and noticed an ambulance there. Captain Stettner was still in his office, with the five men who had gone to the laboratory: the three members of the emergency-squad who had gone there first, and the two men he had taken along with him. They all had their left sleeves rolled up.

He was looking worried. "It's been discovered that one of the smashed canisters contained virulent bacteria of the group . . ." He looked at the doctor, wanting to get it right.

"*Verlanzickerpocken.*" He broke another capsule while the nurse cleaned the next arm. "It isn't serious. No question of quarantine. But precautions are indicated."

I took off my coat. The taint of ether was in the air. "What about the people who raided the place?"

"I have arranged for periodic radio and television warnings," Stettner said. "The evening papers will also carry stop-press announcements." He watched the hypodermic lance into my arm. "The Medical Association and all hospitals are being contacted immediately by cable and telephone, so that if anyone goes to a doctor or a hospital asking for inoculation, the police can be called in to question them." He put his jacket on and spoke to the doctor. "There is no need for any special instructions? We may continue our work as usual?" There are people who, physically courageous, have nevertheless a horror of infection. He was one.

"You can forget about it. If you notice a rash around the genitals in fourteen days, report for medical attention." He signaled for the nurse to pack up the kit. I left soon after them. The evening Bourse would be on the air in thirty-five minutes; it would take fifteen to reach the hotel.

The route led past a stretch of the Wall that I always tried to avoid, but tonight it was quicker for me to go that way. On the pavement below the Wall there were wreaths and dead flowers, because at this point there was a cemetery on the other side, and people tried to throw their tributes over in remembrance of dead relatives in the Eastern Zone.

Passing the place, my sense of oppression increased and I had to make a deliberate effort not to think about Solly, and the look of surprise that he had died with. He had heard my shout, and the bunch of keys had just missed his face, so that he had died surprised, not hearing the shot. With a breech-pressure of twenty tons per square inch, a rifle bullet travels faster than sound. It had drilled his head.

Southward through Kreuzberg I checked the mirror, saw nothing, and rechecked, and finally got bored. It didn't matter if there was a tag. The game had passed beyond that stage.

On my right stood the Schinkel Monument, floodlit, dominating the city, a shining beacon in the night. What did it say? *This is Berlin.* Where and what was Berlin? The capital of a sometime hell on earth, split by a wall and writhing, as a cut worm writhes.

A set of lights changed to red, to green, to red again, and I hadn't moved off on the green. Some bastard was blaring behind me with his horns. Too tired to get out and bash him. Green again. Shove off. Automaton. Birds are winged things, men are wheeled things.

The street ran straight, a bright rainbow running to the black of sky. The buildings leaned back for me and then closed in again. Brakes. Nearly hit a taxi. Foot too heavy on the throttle, going too fast. Slow. Something wrong. Pull up. Breather. People on the pavement.

A man with a quiet face opened the driving door and looked down at me and said: "Shift over." I tried to lift my hand to push him away but there was no strength left.

"Wha'?" I asked him stupidly.

"Shift over. I'll drive."

I dragged my leaden body across to the other seat. Obedience. Worst sin of modern man, obedience.

He got in and slammed the door, pulling into the traffic stream. I sat with my chin on my chest. Last remembered thought: *hypodermic*.

11 | OKTOBER

Her skin was the shade and texture of a wax rose, quite flawless, and her hair fell across her naked shoulder in blond rivulets. Her regard was innocent, the eyes wide and frankly gazing, too young to have learned that you must sometimes glance away. She leaned across the white chair without coquettishness, insouciant, her small breasts barbed with nipples of carmine, her thighs heavy with pubic hair.

The ant cleaned its antennae.

The light in the room came from a great Daum chandelier, and burned on the gold of the frame. It was no good thinking in terms of taste. She was there for raping. They might just as well have hung a whore on the wall. There was no signature, but the painter had been a German, a true blue Prussian-born hypocritical bloody Aryan. You portray the face as symbolizing purity—the flawless skin, the innocent gaze, the little-girl look—and then you go to town on the tits and pussy, symbolizing carnality till it moans. Result: you have a picture you can give to your own mother-in-law for hanging in the needle-room, and she'll always think you've come to admire her petit point.

Hypocrisy. Schizophrenia. They've always been like it. That's why you've got to talk about Beethoven and Belsen in the same breath. You can't think of one without the other.

If you kick over an anthill, the first thing they do is stop and clean their antennae with a foreleg. In their panic they resort at once to habit, to deceive themselves that everything is really all right and the sky hasn't fallen down. The human species is inclined a little that way. Tea in the blitz.

Regaining consciousness in the confines of a trap, I had controlled primitive brain panic by resorting to a habit and criticizing the picture, as if it had been in a cozy gallery along the Kurfürstendamm. But it was no go. You couldn't look at that split-minded perpetration without knowing precisely where you were. Deep in the heart of Deutschland.

The room was large, lofty ceilinged, and encrusted with baroque marble, gilt, silk, and ormolu. Traceries, moldings, *coquillage* and arabesque, brocade and parquetry—there was nowhere for the eye to rest. Hermann Goering would have rolled in here like a pig in clover. No, you couldn't get away from where you were.

The movement of my head had left no dizziness. I had expected to wake from the equivalent of a low sleep-curve, groggy and disorientated; but the drug had no aftereffects. I was sitting in a silk brocade chair with a cushion behind my head, facing the length of the room at whose far end was a pair of white and gold doors. I felt like a minor monarch about to grant privy audience. They did you well here.

My watch read 9:01. Less than an hour since they'd snatched me. They'd followed me away from the Z Bureau, knowing I would pull in somewhere when the drug took effect. No rough stuff, nothing embarrassing.

There were four men in my audience-chamber. One against the doors, one standing with his back to the monstrous Rasputin Quinze fireplace, one staring out of the window, and one coming quietly toward my chair.

"Excuse me," he said in Heidelberg German, and lifted one of my eyelids. He had seen my movements.

I asked him: "How am I?"

He stood back with a faint and charming smile. Elegantly

dressed, crisp white hair, two gold rings, a quiet and melodious tone. "You are very well."

Everyone began moving. The man by the window went down the room to the doors and the man there took a place to one side. They were taking up positions. They were the guards. The man by the fireplace came to join the doctor. I looked up into his face and knew that if I got out of here alive it would be on his terms.

"I am Oktober," he said.

And the mirage dissolved, and all the silk and arabesque and or-molu were gone, and I sat here in a cell. Even the air had gone chill.

I bowed my head. "Quiller," I said.

His eyes were rivets in a face like a steel trap that clanged when the mouth opened and shut. "You may talk."

I took an instant to weigh up the moves. They had a doctor here. I knew what that meant. But there was a computer in operation inside the steel trap. The material was human, therefore it must be handled in human terms. It was invited to talk.

"How are the Z Polizei?" I asked. "Back on the job?"

"They were injected with a neutral fluid."

"It was rather elaborate."

"It was efficient. We didn't want you to give any trouble."

The doctor had moved away. It wasn't his turn. The chill of the air reached my spine.

"And you didn't want me to get hurt. Yet."

"No."

"Then why did you try to crush me against that wall?"

A light gleamed in the eyes and went out. "It was a mistake."

In big organizations the right hand doesn't always know what the left hand is doing. I wondered what had happened to the wild-cat operator who had jumped orders and gone for me against that wall. As a guess he was now hanged, drawn, quartered, cut piecemeal, canned, and on a shelf in the supermarket labeled CAT FOOD.

I studied Oktober. The steel-trap face was deceptively decorated so that a passing glance would accept it as that of a human being. It was oblong, the chin the same width as the forehead. The hair was gummed down flat, Hitler-fashion but without the cowlick. The eyes were flint-gray, with nothing in them but black pupils—no hint of a soul behind. The nose was dead straight. The mouth was dead straight. There was nothing else. I went on looking at it until it spoke again.

"Talk."

I said: "It's turned out nice again."

He might as well know that I would never talk. If anything ever talked, it wouldn't be me. It would be the half-dead remains of the thing called Quiller, jabbering in its death throes. I hoped it would give nothing away. There were people I had to protect. The only guarantee I could give them now was that if I let them down, it wouldn't be Quiller ratting on them, but just a lump of blood and gristle and pain that was beyond knowing what it was doing. I had seen men being interrogated at Buchenwald.

Oktober spoke again.

"We know who you are. In the Churchill war you refused military service. You wasted your time masquerading as a German soldier and trying to sabotage the efficient working of the Final Solution, 'rescuing' Jews and other subhuman organisms from what in fact was their prescribed destiny. You failed in your grandiose intentions. When offered awards by the Polish, Dutch, and Swedish governments after the war, you refused them, thus admitting your failure and your shame. We know about you."

I had worked out the only possible move, and began taking very deep and very slow breaths to feed oxygen into the blood so that it should be available to the muscles. By careful degrees I tensed my arms, legs, and abdomen, and then relaxed. Tense, relax. Tense, relax. Increase oxygen intake, circulation, and muscle-tone.

"You are a known authority on memory, sleep-mechanism, the personality patterns of suicide, critical-path analysis, fast driving techniques, and ballistics. You are known to be at present in the service of M.I.6."

Wrong. Never mind. He was watching my eyes for reaction so that he could get a clue to the truth or untruth of his information. Most of it was correct. I kept my eyes blank. Tense . . . relax.

"You thought we didn't know who was supplying the court with so-called 'war criminals' at Hannover in the past six months. We knew who it was. You were seen in different areas and we built up a *portrait parlant* of you. We recognized you when you went to the Neustadthalle. It was reported that your cover had been called off, so we knew that you were embarked on some more special undertaking. There is very little we don't know about you."

Breathe deep. The window was nearer than the doors but that way out was no go. The heavy curtains were drawn but there was a gap and there was lamplight outside, shining on the bare boughs of a plantain. Its height made a fair reference: this room was three floors up, maybe four. I wouldn't be given time to hunt about for balconies or drainpipes. It would have to be the doors. Tense . . . relax.

"But we lack certain information about your Bureau. We have observed its affairs closely for some time, and we wish to fill in our picture of M.I.6."

Not subtle. The repetition was clumsy, and it was now clear that he was feeding me doctored corn, trying to provoke me into retorting—for pride's sake—that he was wrong, that I wasn't with M.I.6. Eyes blank. Breathe deep.

Oktober riveted me with his soulless eyes. "We must thus oblige you to talk." He was too intelligent to make any threats, because he knew I had seen men interrogated by his kind. There was simply no option but to talk. He said: "Begin."

Tense . . . relax. I must bear in mind that this meeting with this man in this house was the goal of my mission. Certainly the ball had bust the net: I'd hoped to arrive in this house in possession of my senses and with a chance of getting clear before it was too late. The inoculation trick had been elaborate, yet it had involved no more than a phone call to Captain Stettner purporting to come from the Medical Office of Health, a private ambulance, a doctor, and a nurse. Phönix would possess such facilities: one of the accused at Hannover held a chair at the medical faculty of Nürnberg; the hierarchies of more than one ministry were riddled with Nazi executives. The effort of ensuring that I should be brought here insensible had been worth making. But I must bear in mind that my mission had been to expose myself in open ground, draw the enemy fire, and thus locate his base. I had done that. The advantage was mine. This thought must be repeated, to give psychological help to the physical necessity of somehow staying alive and sane.

Breathe deep. Tense, relax. *The advantage is mine.*

Oktober said: "Will you talk?"

I said: "No."

The scene changed a little. At the movement of his hand the two guards came away from the doors and halted within three yards of my chair, each pulling a Münslich 8 mm. flat-butt and flicking the catch. Oktober looked at something behind my chair, and I realized there was a fifth man here. He came into my range of view. He was the doctor who had used the needle on us at the Z Bureau. His surgeon's gown was spotless and his hands moved deftly among the equipment in the kit that was carefully set down on a little Japan-lacquered table by my side. It would be the same hypodermic, I supposed.

The pattern emerged. He was the anesthetist. The older man, finely groomed and noble of face, was the psychoanalyst. No crude torture, then. Just the direct clinical invasion of the psyche.

I had to alter, by a little, the move that must be made. The guards had closed in, making things more difficult but leaving a clear run to the doors once immediate opposition was dealt with. The threat of the guns was minimal: I was fairly confident they wouldn't fire. I was wanted alive. A leg shot to stop me running would be pretty useless if they didn't actually strike a main nerve and paralyze the limb; a man can go on running with a leg wound if he has the will.

I have never carried a gun in peacetime. It is an impediment, physically and psychologically. Some operators clutter themselves up with guns, code books, flashlights, and death-pills. I travel light. A gun is as clumsy as a woman's handbag. It is utterly useless in defense at a distance because you haven't time to draw even if you see the adverse party with his rifle leveled, which you won't. In Solly Rothstein's case I wasn't the target, and I was expecting the shot, and saw the rifle at the window; but I couldn't have picked off the sniper with a revolver at that range except by luck. Psychologically you have the advantage, unarmed, providing the adverse party knows that you are. (These people knew. They would have frisked me on the way here.) Knowing you have no gun they're not afraid of you, and fear is a natural spur to alertness: unarmed, you disarm them. Any demand at gunpoint always carries the risk of failure because they mostly demand that you do something useful to them and you can't do much when you're dead. A gun is psychologically a penis-substitute and a symbol of power: the age-range of toyshop clientele begins at about six or seven, rises sharply just before puberty and declines soon after the discovery of the phallus and its promise of power. From then on, guns are for kids and for the effete freaks and misfits who must seek psycho-orgasmic relief by shooting pheasants.

There are a few special situations when a gun is useful. This wasn't one of them. A gun would have been useless to me now.

Oktober spoke.

"Take off your coat."

The anesthetist was filling the syringe. The fluid was colorless. There looked to be about two ounces.

Stand up. Breathe deep. Slip the coat off. Squeeze the toes, relax them. Remember: *The advantage is mine.* And now the final requisite: rage. The blood needed a shock-dose of adrenalin to anoint sudden intense physical action. *They're after my guts, this arrogant pack of Hitlerite Belsen bastards! A noble death—smeared underfoot by a clique of schizo shits!*

The very action of taking off a jacket sets it up as a weapon because for an instant it is held both-handed like a matador's cape. I let Oktober have it across the face in a blinding shroud and kneed

101

for his groin once and again and found the rim of the little Japan-lacquered table and sent it pitching head-high to a man at the guard on the left, hearing the gun clatter down as the other guard swung a razor-chop left-handed that missed the neck and burned a shoulder blade before I could get a sight of his leg and work on it. The placing was perfect because momentum was taking the weight of my body forward hard and at a low angle so that as my shoulder hit his knee my left hand hooked him behind the ankle (so the foot couldn't shift), and he screamed as the knee-joint broke.

Someone fired but fired to miss and I knew it and kept up the pressure, thrown off-balance now by the collapsing of the guard's leg but getting some of it back with one hand hitting the thick carpet and pivoting me half-round to face the line of run: the doors. The situation seemed comfortable so far: Oktober had staggered back because of the coat, but my knee had found his groin a second time and I'd heard the grunt in his throat and his face would be white by now. One guard out of action with a smashed leg. The anesthetist would be psychologically worried by the wrecking of his equipment and didn't look unarmed-combat-trained anyway. The psychoanalyst wouldn't weigh in, wasn't his field.

I began the run. A foot beside me, the pile was raised by the spit of a wide slug—shooting to miss again because at this range they could have split the spine if they'd wanted to. A word of command from Oktober. My right foot in trouble as fingers locked around the ankle, and I hit the ground halfway to the doors, jackknifing and swinging a buncher at the hands: no go. The table came and I twisted and caught it against the shoulder as the hands bettered their purchase and I had to engage with the guard, using my other foot against his neck and pressing back and back as he yielded, one hand coming away but the other holding on. Switch tactics: let the foot give way and bring his head closer with a jerk. No go again—he'd rolled and put the grip on and I had to kick for the side of the head, getting it once but not hard enough.

A shadow stood over me and an arm locked round my neck and that was it. A final effort and then both legs and the neck were trapped. I waited for the pressure. It didn't come. Oktober was giving commands and I heard the doors shutting: the crash of the table against my shoulder had muffled the sound of their opening.

In a few seconds the arm was unlocked from my neck and my legs were released and Oktober said:

"You may get up."

I was smart about it for decency's sake, and tucked my shirt in, making it look like the end of a dormitory rag. Breathing not too bad, didn't wheeze. Relax.

The little Japan-lacquered table lay in four pieces and the anesthetist was still gathering up his gear. One guard stood behind me: I could feel him there. Six men had come into the room and stood in a ring, each with a gun out. The other original guard was still on the carpet with his leg at a dreadful angle from the thigh and a puddle of vomit beside his blenched face. The psychoanalyst was standing outside the ring of men, looking straight at my face with the intensity of a painter who must commit what he sees to his canvas. Oktober stood stiffly, visibly accommodating his pain and refusing his groin the comfort of his hands. The color was seeping back into his face but the sweat had gathered and dripped from his chin.

The anesthetist had charged a smaller syringe and now stooped over the prone guard, lancing the calf of his leg, straightening up. No one spoke. I could hear Oktober's breathing; the pain was audible in it. My right arm was going numb from the blow of the table and the shoulder blade throbbed. I'd got off lightly; they could have done much worse than this. The guards were well trained: the orders must have been: *He is not to be damaged unless absolutely necessary.*

The anesthetist nodded to Oktober, who said: "Two of you. Take him to Dr. Löwe. Then come back."

The guard was unconscious. They carried him with his legs together. The doors opened and closed. The anesthetist was checking the damage to his kit. Oktober asked him what the situation was, and he said: "We can proceed when you are ready, Herr Oktober."

The five remaining guards were signaled to close in, and Oktober said to me: "Sit in the chair." There was no expression on the oblong face, no hate in the eyes. He would not wipe the sweat from his chin. It wasn't there. The pain wasn't there. I had done nothing to him.

I sat down again in the brocade chair and began thinking out the next move. Oktober said:

"Zander. Take aim at the left foot. Gebhardt, the right foot. Schell, the left hand. Braun, the right hand. Krosigk, aim at the genitals." I watched the little barrels line up. All catches were set at fire. "At the slightest movement, shoot. Do *not* wait for my order." He spoke to the anesthetist. "Approach the patient from behind and work without covering any line of fire." To me he said: "Be careful not to move your hands or feet by the smallest degree, especially when the needle enters."

The smell of ether and soap came into the air as the man passed behind me and rolled up the sleeve of my shirt and cleansed the skin. I looked around me without moving my head. The psychoanalyst was still studying me, assessing his material. The five guards had their eyes fixed on the five targets; their fingers were curled on the triggers. I stopped thinking out the next move. There wasn't one.

"Proceed."

The needle went in.

12 | NARCOSIS

The seven men looked very small but I knew the reason: they had been ordered to post themselves in a line across the doors and put up their guns. Thus it was distance that diminished them, nothing else.

The watch indicated that fifteen minutes had passed since the injection, and I now began checking on visual references: the size of the seven men, the intensity of the light on the gold inlay of the console by the window, the height of the ceiling, other things. There was no question of my having been given a hallucinatory drug: they didn't want an outpouring of hallucinations, but the truth.

The room was very still. The great chandelier hung like a jeweled moon. The men made a tableau: seven guards at the far end of the room, motionless. Much nearer, Oktober, hands behind his back, feet slightly apart, motionless. Nearer still, the narcoanalyst, his stance neat but relaxed, fine head bowed a degree to look down at me, motionless. Beside my chair, the anesthetist, just out of sight.

My only friend was the watch. Now sixteen minutes since the injection. It wasn't my own watch, but his, the analyst's. Too involved with working on me, he failed to take into account that I was working on him, preparing to do what I could against the drug; he therefore made the mistake of folding his arms as he stood gazing at me. When reality starts slipping you must find something real to hold on to, a spar in the roughening sea. Manmade time is real, and measured in precise degrees: you may think an hour has passed, but a watch will correct you if you're wrong. This watch would help me in three ways. It would correct any distorted estimation of the passage of time; it would, in correcting me, warn me that my own time-sense (and therefore the clarity of my wits) was becoming impaired and that an effort must be made to steady up; and it would provide an aid in trying to name the enemy: Pentothal, Amytal, hyoscine, or whatever was now in my bloodstream and lapping at my brain cells. The time element varies greatly in different narcotic techniques.

I couldn't look at my own watch because they'd see me glance down and would realize the danger and take my watch away. I could see the analyst's watch easily and clearly because his arms were folded, and I let my gaze run periodically up and down his figure from head to foot, with sleepy blinks, as if I were feeling the effects of a soporific. In between blinks I checked his watch. Now seventeen minutes.

There hadn't been a sound in the room for seventeen minutes, and now he spoke.

"My name's Fabian." It was said with a shy smile. "I don't know yours."

The anesthetist was perched on a stool beside me and I could now see the white of his gown on the edge of my vision-field. He had strapped a constrictor around my right arm and would be checking my blood pressure as we proceeded, to forewarn himself of any syncope. He was at this moment taking my pulse. He would also be listening the whole time to my breathing.

Genuine indications of sedation began now, so I counterattacked at once, forcing alertness and busying myself with the problem: what was the drug they were using? Certainly it was in the barbiturate group, not the amphetamine: it was sleep-inducing and not stimulative. But Pentothal would have acted faster than this. The first approach by the analyst gave me a clue: I was expected to feel the onset of urgent demands for sympathy with the interrogator. But the effects of any given narcotic vary according to the reaction against it. I would not, on an operating table, want to wrestle mentally with a surgeon who was going to heal me. In this room and in this chair I was prepared to wrestle for my life.

To pin down the drug that was in me, I would have to set up a complicated permutation of effects and reactions *in these circumstances*, and test each possible drug for *assumed* reactions according to the known characteristics of my own personality.

It wasn't worth it.

Steady. It's worth anything. You can kill men if you're not careful, men like Kenneth Lindsay Jones.

The eyelids were heavy. He was watching me, waiting for my answer. The hand of the watch had hardly moved. He had only just spoken. *My name's Fabian. . . . I don't know yours.* Make correction and be warned: five minutes had seemed to pass, within thirty seconds.

Say it sharply, briskly.

"Quiller." Not bad.

"And your first name?"

First names. Sympathy. Only one answer: bollocks.

Said nothing.

Think clearly. If it were Pentothal it wouldn't be too much to cope with. He'd start his questions any minute now, and catch me in the twilight before sleep, off guard, then question me again in the twilight of waking.

Any more clear thoughts? Fabian. I'd heard that name, in the medical world. Dr. Fabian . . . someone. One of the top-kick psychoanalysts. Trust Phönix to use the best.

The light was spangled on the gold face of the watch and a twin spark echoed from the inlay of the console table.

"What's *your* name?" the quiet voice asked.

Said nothing.

He was going to miss. I was going out slowly and there wouldn't be much time to get anything coherent if he didn't start soon.

Might not be Pentothal. Think clearly: what do they want to know? First, my setup, location of Local Control Berlin, names of operators, current code systems, so forth. Second and more vital, the extent of my knowledge about Phönix. Third, the exact nature of my present mission. They wouldn't ask me directly. It would be the classic technique of the leading question aimed at forcing me to dodge and lie and cover up, so that a mere hesitation would give me away. The technique was difficult for extracting names.

"Inga."

My breath hissed and I heard it.

Red sector. I was going under. It had only been a few seconds since he'd asked, "What's *your* name?" Not ten minutes, as it seemed. I'd been concentrating consciously on the need to think clearly (and combat the sedation), and the typical Pentothal reaction had begun subconsciously: hidden psychic material was coming to the surface, pushing past all thoughts of danger and reticence and control. And she was there in the twilight, my lean black *succuba*, uncurling in my mind.

He said without surprise, "Your name is Inga?"

"Yes." Outsmart the bastard.

First onset of doubts: you think you can outsmart this team? A tried and proved narcotic flooding the walls of your will, and a narcoanalyst with an international reputation?

Yes. It had to be yes or nothing.

Eyes were closing. Reaction setting in very fast now so one thing left to be done. She was dominating the id, or I wouldn't have said her name, so let her loose, do what she will, let her queen it over all the other dormant images and see how Oktober would like *that*. He would have to tell his Führer that he couldn't learn anything about the Quiller bureau but he'd learned all there was to learn about her litheness and lightness and darkness in the still rose room that surprised him, the keys in his face, his poor dying face, *Solly look out!*

Elbow slipped. Wink of gold, twin wink of gold, the white of her throat and the men very small, seven small men my name is Quiller and her name is Inga tell you about her tell you all in black so black you long to see the white of her long lean body in black but is she a woman or the life of something dead or still a kid with the stink of burning flesh in the Führerbunker my clever Fabian she's in love with the Führer straddled on the black Skai slabs and rutting with ghosts in the night-beat music, Inga my love my hate, enigma, shadow in body, your body in black and the glass empty to see you again because I have to and have to stroke your skin my love my hated love tell you Fabian you shit *I'll tell you tell you tell you!*

Better than I'd imagined, or worse, with the bitter taste of the aftermath already souring the sweetness and the scent of her heat, long-reaching and straining, no sound but the sound of our breath, nothing to show for it but the slip of sweat and the writhe of limbs, all heady pleasure and the Damoclean blade: she'd rather do this with a short-arse with a small moustache who's dead and a poof to boot, how's that for your pride, my whoring rake-hell! But take what you can and then get out and no regrets but the stain on the Skai and the stain in your mind because you swore you'd never try it and now you have and you can never get back to where you were before, clean of her. Lie still, and lie still under me. Dissociate. You are a woman before you are a bloody necrophile, and I've had you where you are a woman and nowhere else. Now get out, Quiller. Get out. But where will you go?

I was surfacing, but everything was mixed as if three or four negatives were superimposed: her face floated in the frame of the console table, the man in front of me had a mane of silver hair and a small dark moustache; the images of the real and unreal were jumbled. She had scratched me. My upper arm was stinging.

Then the doubts came. What was real? Was anything? The faces floated: Pol's, Hengel's, Brand's—they were faces I had seen only once. Or had I seen them, ever? Who was Pol? Hengel?

Brand? I must have imagined them; they had come and gone without meaning to me. I began being afraid of being mad.

The gold winked on the watch-face. My arm stung. She had—no! The needle . . . not her nails. They'd used the hypodermic again while I was under. Stung. The stuff was flowing in my blood now, creeping toward my brain. A tightness on my other arm. Gasping noise. Not Fabian. Pumping up the constrictor. A hand on my pulse—throw it off! No strength.

The chandelier swam in the sky, a million stars.

Panic, then control: anger. Angry because I'd panicked.

Time—check time! No go. His arms were by his sides, not folded. Dirty trick. A thought came: think out what the sting means. Steady up or they'll have you, Quiller. *Think.*

Pattern was: Past—one injection, effective period twenty minutes, soporific, probably Pentothal. No memory of interrogation except asking for my name. (Problem: why no interrogation? Immediate amnesia?) Present--surfacing from unconsciousness, memory of dream-copulation with Inga, probable verbal running-commentary, no memory of questions. Future—the effects of the second injection and my reaction to them. Terribly important to work out what technique they were using, and so combat its effects. Or try.

"That was a good sleep you had."

Sound helped vision. I was surfacing very fast now, coming up like a rocket from the depths. This wasn't the normal effect of Pentothal. Everything was coming in loud and clear: the light steadied and his face was etched against the moldings of the ceiling; his eyes were luminous. Heartbeat quickening—chest rising and falling—onset of anxiety—

Dear Christ I knew now what they'd done!

"You feel more yourself now, Quiller. Tell me how you feel."

"I feel fine." I'd answered before I could stop myself.

So it wasn't Pentothal. It was the sleep-kick trick: gradual narcosis with sodium-Amytal, then a shock dose of Benzedrine or Pervitine to kick the sleeper awake. My brain was so clear that I could

110

remember the exact words the lecturer had used in 1948: *the brutal awakening makes the verbal objectivization of psychic contents most urgent, so that they come into the speech-phase with an explosive force hitherto unknown.*

My body was shaking and the nerves were tingling as if a network of galvanized wires covered my skin. The light was diamond-bright and the sound of his voice had the clarity of a bell. The strength flowed through my limbs and I wanted to shout with it, with the ecstasy of it, of being so strong. I raised my hand to smash down the chandelier at a blow, and knew that my face had gone slack and stupid because my hand hadn't moved. They'd put straps at the wrists and ankles, knowing how strong I'd be, strong enough to fell ten men. Then the schism came: I was mighty, but powerless to move. I longed to talk, but I mustn't. Result of the schism: anxiety. The tongue tumescent and aching for the orgasm of speech that must be held back. *Hold back.* All you've got to do. *Hold back!*

Battle stations.

"Now you can tell me all you want to, Quiller."

"There's nothing to tell."

"I'm listening—"

"I'm not talking, Fabian. There's nothing to tell you."

"But I'm interested and there's a sympathy between us—"

"Listen you can keep me here till I'm black in the face but it's no go, it's no bloody go!" I'd switched into English but he was with me, switching too.

"We don't want to keep you here long because your Control will be worried about you. You haven't reported for a long time—"

"I don't report, don't have to report, they—" *Hold back!*

"But you can't lose touch with them—"

"There's Post and—"

"Yes?"

"Postman always rings twice." Sweat pouring from under the arms, breathing like a pair of bellows.

"We've told your Control you'll be out of touch with them for a few—"

"You don't have to stamp—stamp your foot, Fabian, I say bloody well stamp your foot, man!" Madness, a kind of madness, you murder and then blurt it out. Switch back into German and try muddling thought-processes. "Listen, there's nothing to tell you—you think you can sit me in a chair and pump me full of dope and expect me to squeal on people like Kenneth Lindsay—Solly Joe, poor Solly Joe it was *my* fault, *my* fault, just as I told him but he didn't hear because he was dead—you think he'll ever forgive me, you think he will, *ever?*"

Shaking all over. Stink of sweat. The schism again but a different kind: perfectly aware, *acutely* aware of what they were trying to do—make me give them names and ciphers and details of mission—yet acutely aware too of the necessity of holding back, of safeguarding lives and the entire existence of the Bureau. And all the time the overwhelming urge to spill it all out and be done with it. It was the schism of the alcoholic: the hand reaching for the bottle and the mind trying to stop it, and failing.

"You don't have to stamp the letters in the post? We know that." A gentle voice, almost hypnotic. "We don't know how you *receive* the signals. That must be very clever, for people not to know—"

"How the hell can people be allowed to know what we're doing when the whole *object* is strict hush? You think our kind of organization could go on running against people like Phönix if half the administration weren't geared to finding out ways of sending and receiving hush-signals without putting Pol in the box and Win—*winter*—winter windsay Jones keeping up with her bloody stinking necrophilia when she leans across like that if you won't tell you I *won't* tell you Naumann the snowman—"

"Winter wind?"

"Stuff it!"

"Oh, *I* know the box you mean—"

"You don't you never went there—"

"Poll? Polling-booth? Box?"

"She's dead bones I tell you—"

"*Jack* in the box? A toy shop? *Spielzeugladen?*"

"Think again . . ."

"You've got me guessing."

"Guess again then Arabian guess again Fabian forgive me Solly my *fault!*"

Acute awareness of danger, acute awareness of drift. No immediate amnesia, knew what they were doing, picked me up on *winter* straight away and dear God help me I let *Pol* come out. Hold back. Or better, let it rip. Main psychic contents, three things: Inga (sex), Kenneth Lindsay Jones (shock of his death) and Solly Rothstein (guilt). Could play on these because they were clamoring for attention and confession. Safe, because two were dead and she was death itself.

Still shaking. Chair like seat in a roaring roller coaster swinging round the sky. Mouth full of tongue and the only thirst was for words—tell, tell, tell! "Flowers on the pavement—I'll throw flowers over the wall for Solly in the event of my death please send this container Flores for Solly Las Ramblas personally—I said *personally*, you hear me, you bloody well hear me?" Shivering and feverish now, swinging along and a hand on my wrist. "*How am I, Doctor? How am I?*"

A glass vase tinkling somewhere near because I'd shouted it loud as I could, bellowed it out at the globe of stars. If only he'd cooperate!

"That's in Barcelona. *We* know that."

"Don't know everything."

"We know the avenue called Las Ramblas, in Barcelona. What number is it?"

"Spanish Inquisition new-style with Amytal these days is it, oh but you're damn clever see the bull-ring, ever see the bull-ring? She stands like a matador feet together and hips forward till you want to horn her like a bull would if she stood like that in a bull-ring but—"

"But we've forgotten the *number* in Las Ramblas—"

"You never knew it and never will—"

"We know it isn't fifteen—"

"Men to mow, men to mow a meadow—"

"We have to send them the *container*, you see, and we don't know the *number*—"

"Go and shit."

"Where is your Control? Not in Barcelona, surely?"

"Keep control."

Keep control. Christ, not easy. Shivering all over blast their eyes he'll never forgive me. Breath like a bellows, slanting light like arrows at the eyes blast their eyes. *You have the advantage.* Use it! Invincible—Quiller the Killer!

The down-curve. I could feel it. The down-curve, glory to God it was coming. I was over the bloody top and on the way down and what had they got? Four names: Pol, Jones, Solly, Inga. Jones dead, Solly dead, Inga mad. Pol left. A dozen Pols in the Berlin directory, fat lot of use to them that was. What else? Post, and stamp, don't have to stamp the letters. In the event of my death. Container. Las Ramblas. A lot of stuff about that lean black cacodemon. Nothing important.

Over the top and on the way down. Play it cool now.

"We'll send the container to Barcelona for you, and your man can pick it up in Las Ramblas. What could be simpler? Just put the number on the container and—"

"Yes yes yes. *Jawort!*"

Say anything. English or German or French. Anything. Watch it, though. Easy does it. In English: "They never got me, though, because I linked up with three others, a Jew and a Dane and a Pole and a Dutchman—*nine* others, that's right. Proper old bean feast—how's your idiom, friend Fabian?" In German: "We are not concerned with reaching a particular line on the map but with the extermination of living forces, in other words plain bloody murder and you know who said that? Hitler the fidget, and may the good Lord rot his soul in hell." In French: "They dropped parachutes that night and Barney got shot dead before he hit the ground. It didn't make any difference, there were ten of us. If we'd—"

"There are two lines of trees, and they sell goldfish and puppy dogs in the middle—now where are we?"

"Las Ramblas."

"Yes, but what number?"

"Five."

"Five?"

"Six. Seven. All good niggers—"

"Fifty-six?"

"*Jawort!*"

Tiring. Splendid sign. The pressure coming off. Everything quite clear, quite lucid, but the fever going.

Fox them.

"*Nona fia buro-ki muldhala im bhano-jhim, sembali vadha.*" Sitting up there with his Fowler's, never get his Litt.D. in Rabinda-Tanath. "*Darmha valthala-mah im jhuma!*" Sense not important. Tree tall, man very dead, fire-cart kill quick, just let it come. No word, oddly, for bullet. "*Varstra-las!*"

"Is that Indian?"

"Ink."

"The American infantry used to take Cotapeeke Indians with them on the battlefield in Normandy, so that orders could be shouted without the enemy understanding them. I expect your Bureau got the idea from that, didn't it?"

"*Burro.* Donkey. Speak Spanish?" Had to answer, *had* to. Verbal diarrhea. Say anything. Urge to speak. Question of time now.

"I always speak Spanish in Las Ramblas, yes. Shall we contact your man in Barcelona by radio for you?"

"They're up a point today. Yesterday they'll—" *Watch it!* "Be boiling over. Look, if you think you're going to—"

"Why are you still in Berlin?" There was an edge on the tone for the first time.

"The new generation is making its breakthrough to a kind of music that has never been heard before. A ballet of intricate patterns that bespell the eye. Try me on—"

"We thought you were flying out—"

"Pigs might fly, phoenixes fly, the higher they fly—"

"Phoenix? Phönix, yes. How did you hear about Phönix?"

"Phone, you tapped my phone, you sods. Listen, there's no talk, no turkey—"

"What was Solly's mission?"

"My fault, *my* fault—"

"What was he researching on?"

"German war, it wasn't fair—"

"Germ warfare? Oh, we know that. But what will your man in Barcelona do with that container?"

Say nothing. Still dangerous: the answers were coming out mixed up because of the need to inhibit them at source, but he was piecing the images together like an expert. He had to open me up soon or it'd be too late and he *knew* that—some of the questions were even direct: what was I doing in Berlin, so forth. Showed he was fighting hard, gloves off.

Coming down the far side now. Worst over. The tingling on the skin had stopped. Sweat drying on me. Anxiety on the wane, normal lucidity returning (more real than the glaring superlucidity of the hepped phase).

He said: "We've just had a call from your Control and you are ordered to make an immediate report. Begin, Quiller."

Then I was out again, whole, and still sane.

There is a dawn area coming between the nightmare rollercoaster phase and the daylight of normalcy, and I was in it now, and knew it.

"Begin your report, Quiller!"

Physically I was all right: a shoulder bruise and some thirst, that was all. Psychically stable: disinclination to plan anything, sense of loss (psychic contents had been spilling), nothing worse.

I could make a check now, and defeat the last enemy, my own disinclination to plan anything. I had to plan. If I were going to live, it'd be on my wits.

The guards were still strung across the far end of the room with their guns out of sight. Oktober hadn't moved. I got a look at the gold wrist watch as Fabian turned to look at him. 10:55. It had been a ninety-minute ride, then.

Start thinking. Why had Fabian turned to look at Oktober? They were both moving away from me to stand halfway down the room. I heard them murmuring. Nothing intelligible. So they'd given it up. Fabian had been reduced, in the end, to trying simple extortion: *Begin your report!* Hoping to tap some remnant source of psychic response. No go.

The room was still and no one moved. The murmuring went on. The smell of ether was on the air, and the taint of the guard's vomit. I wasn't thinking about anything. But I must. Make an effort. Why wasn't I thinking about anything?

Because I knew.

It was the only thing they could do.

Oktober had turned and was coming toward me. He stopped and stood looking down at me. His hands were clasped behind him and the eyes had the stare of glass; and I remembered a man who had stood like this, neatly tailored in black, his hands behind him, saying, *I am due back in Brücknerwald in one hour, for luncheon.* The stamp was on all of them, and it was most marked when they were about to do what this one was to do now.

He said thinly: "You have wasted my time. That is unforgivable."

I watched him turn and go down toward the line of guards. He didn't raise his voice but I heard what he was saying to them. "Schell. Braun." Two of them stepped forward. "He will be given a final injection. When he is unconscious, you will take him by car to the Grunewald Bridge. Shoot him in the back of the neck, and drop him over."

13 | THE BRIDGE

There was a bar still open in the Müllerstrasse and I went in and sat with a rum grog, cupping my hands round the glass and watching the steam. The *Kellner* had gone back behind the bar and looked at me over the coffee-machine for a few minutes before giving it up.

I pressed the long spoon against the slice of lemon, watching the bubbles. The scent of the rum was heady and I breathed it in. Over in the corner a couple of kids sat canoodling, and a thin man was drooped across a table by the window trying to outstare his despair. There was no one else. At this hour of a winter night the bar was a refuge for lovers and the lost, and being neither, I was the only stranger here. When it was cool enough not to scald my lips, I swallowed the grog and asked for another.

The worst of the shivering had stopped. Every time it tried to set up again, I damped it out and sat slack with every muscle relaxed. There was a lot to think about and my body would have to stop demanding my attention; it could count itself lucky to be alive anyway.

My soaked clothes steamed on me.

I was unconscious before they took me from the house. There had been no way of avoiding the last injection because my hands and feet were strapped to the chair. The shot took half a minute to work and I sat there watching them. Oktober stood looking down at me. The two guards came the length of the room and halted near him, waiting for me to slump. In those thirty seconds I did all I could against the drug, knowing that if I let it win, my last hope would go. The anesthetist came around the chair and eyed me impatiently, and I knew that the reaction-time must be five or ten seconds. I'd stretched it to thirty and he was worried. Then the dark came down, on a final consoling thought: *There's nobody who'll miss me.*

Period of total blank.

Death is black and cold and I knew I had died. The waters of Lethe lapped at my feet. But life, returning, was worse, because of the cold. It was colder than death. My face was pressed to the earth and I lifted it and saw the lights along the bridge. A few sick seconds of irrational thought: then there's a life after death and it looks just the same, so forth, then the shivers began and I lay there shaking and clawing at the earth. Inside every dying man there's a live one trying to get out.

The bullet still hurt and I couldn't turn my head. When I'd crawled far enough to get my legs out of the icy water, I raised one hand and felt for the neck wound. There wasn't one. The pain began fading, once I realized that it was imaginary. "Shoot him in the back of the neck," he'd said, and the subconscious had brooded about it, taking the word for the deed.

Short period of nausea. Lay there panting and shaking with the breath hissing against the frosted soil: life, however cheap, comes as a gift when you think you've lost it, and the mind has to make the effort of acceptance.

Ten minutes' hard thinking. I decided to go back among the living as unobtrusively as I could. They had driven me here in the VW and it stood not far off; they had run it clear of the road across the grass. I crawled along the bank of the lake, away from the car, and stood up in the shadow of the bridge. There was no point in checking the speedo-trip because I'd been too dopey to take a reading when the man had climbed in and said he would drive, and even if I'd taken a reading it wouldn't tell me anything: they could have made a detour to the house and/or a detour coming away from it. The most accurate trip-check would tell me only that the house lay within an area of a given number of square kilometers, useful enough in the Black Forest but no good in Berlin.

Tried running-on-the-spot to make warmth but found I was limping. No pain in the leg. Discovery: shoe missing. Limped under the bridge and along the bank on the other side, shaking like a marionette, hands blue in the lamplight.

The rum was spreading through me. It had saved lives at sea and it saved mine now. The *Kellner* had stopped watching me. I'd told him I had slipped on the ice and fallen into the lake but he didn't believe me because I didn't look drunk, just half drowned. Unfortunately he had small feet, otherwise I would have made him an offer for a pair of shoes.

After a while, the shivering stopped and I began going through my pockets. Nothing was missing.

"I'd like a taxi."

He used the phone.

The driver looked wary when he saw me, and held the note against the light. I said: "It's a good one but it just needs putting in a toaster for five minutes. I fell in a lake. Get me some shoes, can you?" He drove me to the rank and did some business with his colleagues and brought me shoes. I left him and walked for two hours at a fast pace from Grunewald to Siemensstadt and back south to Wilmersdorf to get the blood circulating again—and there was no tag.

There was no tag, and it was twenty-four hours before I realized that this one fact sent me along a line of false reasoning that pitched me straight into the red sector again. This night my psyche had been forced to withstand the effects of sodium-Amytal, Benzedrine (or Pervitine), invasion by interrogation, the certainty of death, Pentothal (or a similar knock-out dose), immersion in water near freezing-point, and the shock of returning life. It explains my failure to understand why there was no tag on the fast walk to Siemensstadt and back to Wilmersdorf: the mind was not yet clear enough to think safely. It explains but does not excuse. There is no excuse for carelessness. I should have noted the fogginess of my mind and waited till it was alert enough to make safe decisions. I didn't.

The hotel was called the Zentral and I booked in because despite its name it was buried among a maze of small streets in the Mariendorf district, some eight kilometers south of Wilmersdorf. The place was smaller than the Prinz Johann and less efficiently run: a tousled night porter and dust on the lamp bulbs; and this suited me because it might be necessary to stay officially dead for a time.

My still-wet clothes went unnoticed. *Ja*, there were some lock-up garages. I said I would leave my baggage in the car and bring it in tomorrow morning, as I was tired. He didn't bother to ask where the car was now parked so that an eye could be kept on it. I went ostensibly to bed, locked the door, stripped, showered, and spread my clothes to dry by the radiators. The room was small but clean and well heated, a kinder resting place for this night than the cold dark of the lake.

Immediate sleep was not permissible because the situation had to be worked out first.

I had missed the late-evening Bourse from Eurosound because I'd been on the way to the Prinz Johann to pick it up when they'd made the snatch. Likelihood: no important signal from Control. Nor had I anything to send in. They might find the name of Dr. Fabian ———, psychoanalyst, in the Berlin directory (in missions of this kind when complicated shadowboxing was the rule for both sides, it was sometimes overlooked that a man could be found simply by knocking on his door instead of casting an undercover dragnet for him), and they might start an inquiry on him if I suggested it. The Z Commission could be urged to make a snatch and send him for trial at Hannover as a war criminal. He was working for Phönix somewhere near the top level and it was likely that his wartime record would provide evidence enough to charge him. But I might be able to use him myself to better purpose: through him I could reach Oktober and finally Heinrich Zossen, my main target. Decision: don't signal Control to flush him.

I pulled one of the armchairs near the bed and sat with my feet at head-level, to feed the nerves while I worked. Major question: why was I still alive?

Supposition number one: the guards had driven me to the bridge as ordered, taken me out of the car, held me ready for dropping over, and had been disturbed at the last moment by people, possibly a police patrol. They had simply dropped me as I was (alive instead of dead), unable to risk the sound of a shot. The best laid schemes could go like that. The sound of the splash had to be risked, if a greater risk were that of being seen carrying me back into the car. (Query: Why had Oktober chosen the Grunewald Bridge? There were more secluded places.) So the job had been done at half-cock and they'd reported to Oktober that it had in fact been done in every accordance with orders, relying on the plunge into icy water to kill me before the drug wore off and I could try to swim. They wouldn't report the truth, that I hadn't been shot in the neck, because Oktober would flay them.

Findings of supposition number one: Oktober believed I was now dead. The guards were almost certain. Therefore my case was closed and there would be no one tagging me. Confirmation: there had been no tag, either from the lake to the bar or along the Grunewald-Siemensstadt-Wilmersdorf route. Had there been one I would have known it.

Supposition number two: Oktober had tried the double-think on me. He'd wanted me to think that he thought I was dead, so that I would at once go to ground, change my open tactics, and lead him to my base. He had therefore ordered the guards to simulate a killing; they had dipped me into the water and left me on the bank so that I'd believe I must have swum, half conscious, to safety and then passed out again. I would be expected either to think they hadn't been able to shoot me (for reasons as in supposition number one: interruption) or to be so thankful for finding myself alive that I wouldn't question it.

Objection: I wasn't likely to lead Oktober to my base unless they put a strict tag onto me, and they hadn't done that. Query still insistent: why the Grunewald Bridge?

Supposition number three: Oktober had threatened me with death in the hope that fear would work where the narcotics hadn't. He was too subtle a man, and knew my wartime experience among the death camps too well, to make it an open threat. He had goosestepped up to me, stood in the living stance of the typical Nazi executioner, and rapped out the Hitlerite announcement about unforgivably wasting his time. Leaving me, to speak to the guards, he hadn't raised his voice, because he knew I would hear and thus hoped I would believe in what I heard: my own sentence of death. There are many and distinct types of courage and fear. A man who will climb the face of a cliff may funk grasping a snake; a man who will brave a raging sea may faint at the sight of blood. Oktober might have hoped that a man who with his hands free was prepared to attack five others and go on attacking even when shooting began would lose his spirit once his hands were tied and he was made to overhear the cold hard details of his certain death.

So I had been meant to talk, to save myself. They'd failed but must not admit it. The charade had been performed: the dope, the car journey, the dumping. Oktober was shown to mean what he said. (Again, I was expected to reason as in supposition number one and satisfy myself that they had *intended* to kill me.)

Objection: they would have tagged me from the lake. But the query was answered now: they'd chosen the Grunewald Bridge (Oktober had carefully named it in my hearing) so that I should remember the death of Kenneth Lindsay Jones, who had died in the same lake. Intention: to increase my fear and my belief in their purpose, by reference to a similar killing.

There were only two major facts matchable with the three suppositions. One: I was alive. Two: there was no tag. Fact number one matched all three suppositions. Fact number two matched only the first.

The wallpaper, a faint lilac trellis pattern, began swimming in front of my eyes. The need for sleep was now urgent. It would have to rest there for the night: the second supposition was attractive, and it could be combined with the third: they had tried to frighten me into talking, and when that failed they dumped me so that I would lead them to base; but they would have had to follow up. The absence of tag must rule. They thought I was dead.

The lilac trellis brightened and faded. I had to check to see that I had locked the door: further evidence of fatigue. Sleep.

I phoned the police first thing and reported a gray Volkswagen abandoned near the Grunewald Bridge. If Phönix were keeping watch on it for any reason unknown to me, they would see it was the police, and not I, who took the car away. I was dead.

Toothbrush, shaver, two shirts, socks, so forth. I left them at the Hotel Zentral and went to the Hertz office, hanging about for a time until the lunch-shift clerk took over. She hadn't seen me before. I chose a BMW 1500 LS saloon by Michelotti. The name was Schultze, number three passport: there was a millionth chance that Phönix might check to see if I'd re-hired.

Lunch at the hotel, quite the tourist, a brand new valise in my room, and a car in the lock-up.

Then my afternoon began. There is an innocence in the very word "afternoon." Morning is for trains and business and hangovers, night is for love and burglary. The afternoon is the halcyon, the calm coming between earnestness and drama. In Berlin it is a time for cream buns, and the cafés swarm, even on a winter's day. But in Berlin there is, beneath this surface, a tide that runs darker than hell itself, that carries people into tributaries not of their choosing. I was on this tide.

There was a simple force propelling me northward into Wilmersdorf, and it never crossed my mind to deny it.

14 | LIBIDO

She prepared Lapsang Souchong and served it with chips of orange peel in small black bowls, kneeling on the floor to drink; we drank in the manner of a ritual. Sometimes she moved, for no reason other than to let me watch her, knowing it pleased me.

A winter sun was in the sky and a ray of it struck through the window, gilding her helmet of hair. It was very quiet, and when she moved I could hear the fabric of her clothes sliding over her skin. To each his aphrodisiac, and she knew mine. She made no secret of hers.

"Sometimes I can tell a man who has killed others. I know that you have."

"Yes."

"I don't mean in war."

"No."

"What does it feel like?"

"Disappointing."

"Not the thrill you expected?"

"I never do it for thrills. It's always a matter of life, his or mine. It's disappointing because all the urgency goes."

"Like," she said, "when a mouse dies. The cat has nothing left to play with, nothing that moves."

This was why she went to the Neustadthalle: to watch men who had killed others.

We sat in silence drinking tea in the innocent afternoon. She asked me what I had seen in the death camps and I didn't tell her. It was no good thinking that if this wingless vampire had ever spent a day in a death camp she wouldn't be so keen to talk about it now. She was part masochist, and in her pain there'd be pleasure. We talked about the Führerbunker. She liked that. It was no good thinking that this was a prelude to love. There would be nothing of love. This was the prelude to something that we would each act out for our own reasons: the simple biological urge to impregnate and be impregnated, the needs of dominance, subjection, identification, a lot of things known and unknown, an act of catharsis to let the fiends come out and perhaps to let others in. The beast with two backs would lord the jungle for a time, then it would die, without knowing why it had lived.

The small black bowls were empty, and she was trembling, so imperceptibly that only the gold links of the chain on her wrist gave sign of it. There had been nothing said, but she stood up and the ray of the winter sun threw her shadow across the wall as she went into another room, and when she came back she was naked.

Better than I'd imagined, or worse, as it had been in the Amytal dream that we now relived, but with new dimensions that surprised me: most men think they know it all and most do not. It was impossible for me to think that the things she did could have been done by any other woman, though I had known them before. The doer matters more than what is done, and she was Inga, gold of hair, unique and measureless, sometimes whispering to me of things more naked than even her body was, the brittle Berliner accents whittling the air as she opened herself and let the fiends come out, and when the ray of the sun had gone from the wall her tears were drying on me.

And now get out, Quiller, get out, the Amytal had said, but I stayed until the lamps came on in the street and the room glowed with their light. In the mirror of the bathroom my face looked much the

same, though we sometimes fear the identity has suffered change
by its exposure. I heard the bell ring, muted by the door between,
and heard her receiving someone. When my tie was straight I went
through into the living room and saw Oktober standing there, and
knew that since I had left the Grunewald Bridge my reasoning had
been false and that it had led me here. Under the Amytal I had
done, in a dream, what I had come here this afternoon to do; and I
had given Fabian and Oktober a running commentary. *She'd rather
do this with a short-arse with a small moustache who's dead and a poof to
boot . . . You are a woman before you are a bloody necrophile . . .* And I'd
already given them her name. Inga. A thousand Ingas in this fair
city, but only one of them in love with a dead Führer. They knew
which one, and they knew where I'd heard the name Phönix.
(*Phoenix? Phönix, yes. How did you hear about Phönix?*)

The unaudible discussion between Fabian and Oktober was now
as clear to me as if I had heard every word.

Fabian: "We shan't get anything out of him this way."

Oktober: "Then we shall give him special treatment."

"It shouldn't be necessary, and you stand to lose him. If he
talked at all he would be so far gone that you might not get anything intelligible. You might have difficulty in reviving him for further use."

"Advise me, then."

"I saw your reaction when he mentioned the name 'Inga.' You
know her. Who is she?"

"A defector."

"Locatable?"

"Yes."

"Then let him go to her."

"He might not."

"He will. His libido will drive him to her. He'll want to do in reality what we have just heard him dream of doing. His urge to go
to her is overwhelming, and we can even increase it to make it certain. You notice his fear of death: he harped on Kenneth Lindsay
Jones and Solomon Rothstein. We shall play on that fear. Let him

believe he is about to die, and let it be done convincingly. Then give him back his life and let him experience its shock effect. The life-force will surge back and the libido will become all powerful. He will go straight to her."

"I'm not convinced."

"You must accept my word. I made a study of these mechanisms during the war. In hospital wards it was noted that night-loss among severely wounded was always very high within hours of their being told that the operation was successful and that they were going to live. In my own work at the resettlement centers of Dachau and Natzweiler we developed a highly successful technique. We put a man under threat of imminent death for three days, then led him to a gibbet and placed the cord round his neck. An officer arrived to 'save' him at the last minute, countermanding the order to execute. We then closeted him with an expert interrogator—a young female, of course—who withheld the means of sexual relief until he had talked. We learned more from these subjects than by any other methods: and they were men who were quite prepared to go to their death in silence."

"You believe this one would follow the pattern?"

"No. Not this one. But I promise you he'll go to the woman Inga, within hours. In a way he is in love with her. So you will know where to find him, and when you have found him you know what to do."

And my reasoning had been false, *because there'd been no tag.* A tag hadn't been necessary. They'd known where to find me. But they'd do nothing, now. Nothing to me.

Oktober stood in the middle of the room. There were three men with him. One was backed against the door where they had come in. The second guarded the door to her bedroom. The third now moved behind me and blocked the bathroom. The windows could be left unguarded: the tops of the street lamps were below the level of this room. The three men would be armed but their guns were holstered. Between Oktober and myself it was tacitly accepted that a gun offered no threat, because I knew that my life was to be preserved until I had talked. There was of course no hope of getting out of here. Each guard was my weight and half again.

I watched Inga. She showed her fear in a way precisely in line with her character: there was delight in it. Yet it was fear, for all that. She knew who these people were. They were Phönix.

I was waiting for her to look at me, and when she did I glanced upward and down again briefly. It was no go, because even if she could call the wolfhound it would have to smash the opaque glazing of the door that led into her bedroom from the roof stairs, and even if it were trained well enough to open the second door from the bedroom into here they'd shoot it dead on sight. But I had reminded her that Jürgen was not far away, to give her courage.

Oktober said to her: "You should not have left us. More important, you should not have consorted with the enemy. How much have you told him?"

I said: "Nothing."

He didn't look at me. He looked all the time at her. He asked: "How much has *he* told *you?*"

"He's not the enemy," she said. The links of her wrist chain trembled in the glow of the Chinese-moon lamp. "He works with the Red Cross."

He dismissed this without expression and looked at last at me. "You know the situation. We're not going to do anything to you. But you will of course answer my questions when you can no longer stand it. That is inevitable. So it would save time and distress if you accepted the situation immediately."

I felt my left eyelid begin flickering.

"Ask your questions," I told him. "Give me the whole lot, so that I can think about them. We might do a deal."

I was going to interrogate *him*, in silence, and I knew he knew it. He could give me valuable information: each of his questions would tell me how much he knew of me and how much he didn't. And he and I both knew that he couldn't refuse to do as I asked, because if he refused it would be an admission of his uncertainty that he was master. He must convince me that he was master, and that whatever information he gave me would be useless to me because I could never pass it on to my Control before I died. But it was difficult for him. If he agreed, and put his questions on the table, would I take it as a sign of his complete self-assurance, or as the mere false evidence of a self-assurance that he didn't feel? He could do nothing about my findings.

I watched his eyes and he watched mine. Both he and I had dealt with men of our own kind often enough. This was not new to us. The situation was precisely defined: he couldn't let me out of here alive, and he couldn't kill me before I'd answered all his questions. In the interrogation under narcoanalysis, Fabian had asked hardly any questions directly. All his questions had been the result of things I had already spoken about—Las Ramblas, the container, so forth. There had been only one direct question of major concern: *Why are you still in Berlin?* That was when he saw that I was coming out of the narcosis, and he'd put that question in a kind of desperation, with an edge on his voice for the first time.

Oktober would now put direct questions, and expose the extent of his knowledge of me and the extent of his ignorance.

He said: "You are not in a position to do a deal."

"I'm waiting."

Inga had moved and leaned against the wall, watching me. Did she know what was going to happen? She must know. She was versed in these matters by her trips to the Neustadthalle.

Oktober was saying suddenly: "What is your present mission? Is it to find more so-called war criminals for the courts? Why have you begun operating without cover? What was the information that Rothstein wanted to give you when he was prevented? What is your precise objective? That is all."

I was disappointed in him. He knew quite well that once the thing began he'd ask more than that. Where was Local Control Berlin? What total sum of information had Kenneth Lindsay Jones passed to Control before he died? What were the names of—oh, there'd be many questions like those.

"Don't fool about," I said.

His flint-gray eyes registered nothing. "Those are the questions."

There was nothing I could do about it. He'd offered a token bargain. If those weren't his only questions I couldn't prove it. I was now obliged to do a deal: but he was right. I was in no position. I said: "Here are the answers."

No reaction. He didn't believe me.

"One. My present mission is to get all possible information about Phönix and pass it to my Control."

He already knew that.

"Two. If I find more war criminals for the courts, it'll be as a means to an end, to expedite the main mission."

Inga had moved, and a man moved, and she was still again.

"Three. I've begun operating without cover because I prefer to. Cover can become dangerous. I told my Control to leave me a clear field and they did that."

Now I had to talk about something I didn't even want to think about, ever again.

"I don't know what information Dr. Solomon Rothstein would have passed to me if you hadn't prevented him. I think you have some idea about it, because you took immediate steps."

And may God rot your soul.

"Lastly, my precise objective is to flush the prime mover of the Phönix organization and deal with him as I think fit."

He kept his eyes on me. I gazed at their glass.

"How did you first hear the name Phönix?"

"It's a big organization and you can't hope to keep it under cover—"

"Did she tell you?"

"Who?" It was just that I disliked his manners.

"This woman."

"Fräulein Lindt would hardly be so unwise as to talk to strangers, and that's all I am to her."

"Who is the 'prime mover' of this alleged organization?"

"I don't know. The only name I know is yours."

"Where is your Control in Berlin?"

"The deal was that I should answer those questions you first put to me."

He said to the man nearest Inga: "Take her into the next room and leave the door wide open." So that was it and I knew the deal was lost, as I'd known it must be.

She moved before the man could touch her, and looked into my face as she passed me. I said, "Don't worry." The door to her bedroom was opened by the guard there.

The sweat began.

I told Oktober: "You'll lose."

He spoke through the doorway. "Unclothe her."

I knew that he wouldn't have started the thing in this way if Fabian hadn't convinced him on the subject of my libido. They didn't have to undress her to do what they were going to do, but I was to be put under a double strain: the pity for a fellow human who suffered pain, and the outrage of the male animal whose mate is its possession.

She made a sound, something like anger. She had moved into the bedroom before the guard could touch her; therefore she would probably elect to undress without his help. I could hear the fabric against her skin, as I had heard it a few hours ago, but now with different feelings.

I said: "The position is this." I waited until he looked at me. "If I can't stand it, and talk, there can't be any half measures. I'd have to talk totally. That's obvious. If I talk, it'll mean putting my Control right into your hands: the local base, names of operators, communication system, the whole lot. Do you for a moment imagine I'd do that?" The sweat was on my face now and he was watching it gather. The body was giving away the mind, and the mind would have to compensate for its own exposure, and say what it had to say with utter conviction. "There's not much pity in people like us. We're like doctors. We can't do the job if we let pity into it. You know that. So you're going to lose. I'm not talking. Not one word.

Not one word. Do what you like to her, kill her off slowly, let me listen to her dying in there, and take your time, make it last and watch me sweat it out. You won't get a word. Not one word. And when that's failed, you can start on me and do the same with me, fingernails, the thumbs, the urethra, the eyeballs, give me the full treatment, give me the lot. But you won't get a word. Not one word."

He said to the man in there: "Switch on the other lights. All of them."

Faint shadows came against the wall. In here, only the Chinese-moon lamp was burning, a glow. The lights in the bedroom were brighter. I saw the shadow of the man stoop over the bed.

"Begin," Oktober said.

I thought: she's arrived in a death camp at last. It doesn't have to be secondhand any more. Now she'll know.

The shadow was moving. I folded my arms and stood with my head turned to watch the shadow, so that Oktober could see I was watching it. He knew also that I was listening. He watched my face.

I hadn't convinced him. Even if I had, I knew he'd go on with this thing, for the pleasure of it. He was on the borderline between reason and the lusts of the psyche, the line that is crossed sometimes by the schoolmaster who begins caning a boy to discipline him and ends by drawing blood.

I should say something to her, but there was nothing to be said.

The shadows moved suddenly and the man gave a grunt and his arm came up and she cried out and he stood still again. There would be blood on his face from her nails. In there, in the room with the silk sheets and the pile rug and the decorative lamps, was the jungle.

I watched the shadows because Oktober wanted me to. On the Dutch frontier there had been a selection camp that I remembered too well. Those who waited in line had been made to watch those who went before them; but there had been a rough screen made from a tablecloth (I remember the half-circular stain on it, made by a wineglass) and rigged up on a broomstick so that those who waited could see only the jerk of the rope above the screen and the jerk of the feet below it. Because the imagination, once let loose, can be more searing than the shape of the thing witnessed; and this was known and exploited.

There is a typicality to this breed of men that stamps them: the way they will stand with their hands behind their backs to speak death into the faces of the weak, the way they will take quick offense, like schoolgirls, and announce a slight as "unforgivable," the way they will show you only half of horror so that your imagination can run riot and bring you to self-made madness. Thus I was to watch only shadows.

"No don't!" And of course to listen.

I could feel the blood draining from my face. It was a moment before I could place a new sound. The click of a closing manacle. She was no longer free.

She began wailing softly.

Oktober watched me.

We are not gentlemen. We are trained, though, to respect the rights of the citizen in whatever country. If we need transport urgently we are trained to get it in whatever way we can that doesn't encroach on the rights of the citizen: we don't simply steal a parked car even knowing that we shall return it after use. London is very finicky on this kind of thing. Nor do we intentionally involve members of the public in our affairs.

I had transgressed. I had involved Inga. Not intentionally, but London would decree that it had been intentional by negligence: I had known she was a defector from Phönix and therefore connected with the subject of my mission, however negatively, and should have kept away from her. I was directly responsible for this. I must therefore do what I could about it.

I must not stand by and let her suffer pain that would send her mad before she died. I must not give my Control and its purpose and its lives into enemy hands.

Normal resources were unavailable to me. There was no hope of getting out of here and running for it, so that they would leave

her alone. There was no hope of reaching her without being re-
strained by their weight of numbers. I could say nothing to Oktober that would save her, without costing the lives of Control
operators and defeating the Bureau's purpose, which was to safeguard human life on a larger scale against the risks of a resurgence
of Nazi militarism and its war potential.

Of a dozen possible actions, two alone were worth the consideration, and one of those was denied me. It was the first time I had
ever regretted my insistence on traveling light, unencumbered by
the bric-a-brac for which some agents have a fondness—guns,
code books, death-pills, so forth. It would be the complete answer
to this situation: a death pill. Five seconds, and there'd be proof at
Oktober's feet that nothing they could do to her would make me
talk. I carried no pill.

The shadows moved and I watched them and heard the sound in
her throat and knew it was something like the word *please* and that
it was said to me and not to them because they couldn't help her
and she thought that I might.

Oktober watched me. He called through the doorway: "Increase
treatment."

She made another sound and I did the one thing that held out
any hope.

15 | BLACKOUT

I fainted.

The last conscious memory was of Oktober reaching out to save my hitting the floor. It was probably instinctive. I was able, before blacking out, to note that he must be ignorant of the processes of syncope, or he wouldn't try to keep me upright. The longer I remained upright, the longer I would remain blacked out.

Psychological and physical factors were all to my advantage. Although he was ignorant of the actual mechanism of syncope, he would know that I was psychologically conditioned to it, because this was a crisis: I was helpless in a situation of rapidly increasing strain, and however much the ego and superego tried to rationalize and seek comfort or simply acceptance, the id knew I was in bad trouble and was ready to throw the switch and relieve the strain by blacking me out. There was also a psychological lever working in Oktober himself: fainting is considered a sign of weakness, though wrongly (the Guards trooping the Colors are far from weak specimens, however often they fall over; long and motionless standing is a classic physical cause of syncope), and I was Oktober's enemy. In a given case we always tend to believe what pleases us, even when evidence to the contrary is stronger. In this case there were two kinds of evidence presented to him. One: the blackout was shown to be produced falsely, at a time when I was obviously desperate for a way out. Two: it was shown to be produced because I was weak. The former evidence was the stronger, because intelligence agents don't pass out so easily in a crisis: crisis is their *raison d'être* and it is what they live and sometimes die for; otherwise they'd take up dairy farming. But Oktober would accept the evidence that pleased him personally: that the blackout was caused by weakness in his enemy.

The physical factors were to my advantage because they, too, helped to give credence to the genuineness of the faint. The room was very stuffy due to airlessness and the rise of temperature. The central heating was on, and during the last fifteen minutes the temperature had been boosted by the presence of four extra people, each of whose bodies was running at 98.6 degrees F. and throwing off excess heat. My face was bright with sweat and my breathing heavy: two symptoms precursive to a faint.

I was thus psychologically and physically conditioned for the occurrence, and Oktober was furthermore ready to believe the evidence of weakness in an enemy. It was vital that the blackout should look genuine *in its inception*. It was certainly genuine in its *performance*.

The same factors that presented evidence of truth were to my advantage in another way: they helped me to induce unconsciousness. Lack of oxygen, mental strain, so forth. To induce syncope at will in a normal environment is not so easy. The instinctive fear of achieving the desired result—unconsciousness—works against the determination to do it. An advanced student of yoga can induce a form of syncope by one of several asanas, most simply by savasana; but the resulting unconsciousness is salutary, and both body and mind realize it: there is no distortion of any function. I knew that in this crisis a blackout would be salutary indirectly (it would save another's pain), but the body is selfish and will look after only its own direct needs. It was therefore necessary to simulate functional disbalance.

I wasn't worried that my enemy was watching me. The trappings of the trick would look genuine, simply because they *were* genuine. I filled my lungs, blocked the throat and tried to force air out against the block. The face would gradually suffuse as the blood was driven to the surface. Then I emptied the lungs totally, showing gradual and *comparative* pallor. The intrathoracic pressure was rising fast and reaching well beyond the 100 mm. Hg produced by a normal cough, and the pressure was being transmitted to the internal jugular vein and cerebrospinal fluid. In the final seconds of consciousness I tracked the process mentally, to encourage the will. Peripheral filling was now setting up and I could feel the increase of the forearm volume. Cardiac input and output were being reduced, and I held breathing as long as possible to keep the process going.

Then I went slack and inhaled, to bring down the blood pressure with a bang.

The ears sang and the vision lost focus, and the room was darkening as I saw Oktober's hand come out to grab me as I collapsed. The main operation had taken some five or six seconds and I would be blacked out for perhaps ten or fifteen, and even more if he kept me upright instead of putting my head below heart-level.

The blackout was total for a few seconds, then lifted and returned in decreasing waves as the body tried to surface and the mind forced it down again. Various impressions: dark and light, constriction beneath the arms as my jacket was drawn upward by his suspension (he had grabbed it at the front), singing in the ears, muted voice of a man, urgent desire for air, so forth. And all the time the thought: *It's this or nothing, it's got to work.* The mind had been preset to work against the body's recovery, reversing the norm.

Voices again. Inga called something. Water running somewhere. A flash of light as Oktober brought the back of his hand across my face. I was moaning. The shock of the water as they flung it against my eyes. Full consciousness came back and I had to feign continuance of the syncope, letting my dead weight hang on their hands as they tried to wake me, letting my lids droop and the eyes turn upward. My heart was pumping to restore the lost pressure.

They tried a trick and let me fall, and I didn't try to save myself but dropped in a heap and got to my knees and hung on all fours shaking my head to clear it, opening my eyes and saying softly and monotonously, "Carry on treatment ... burn her alive ... you won't get a word, *not one word ... not one word ...*"

Someone closed a door and nobody spoke. I swung my head and tried to focus, blanking the eyes of full intelligence: a man's legs still against the entrance door, Oktober gone, where had he gone? A man behind me, could see his shoe. "Not one word," I said to his shoe. The remains of the water dripped from my face.

Nobody did anything. No one spoke. I got upright and stood swaying, trying to find my pocket, missing, trying again and getting out my handkerchief, wiping my face—the guard by the door had pulled his gun as fast as a snake's tongue and was ready with it, but he knew I wasn't armed; it was his instinct.

A door opened and I heard her sobbing. A shadow loomed on the wall and I saw the arm lifting. It was a low-powered rabbit-chop and I dropped like a sandbag, out before I hit the floor.

The time-sense was groggy but I couldn't have been out for long. The pile of the carpet formed an expanse of high terrain in front of my eyes because the side of my face was lying on it. There were no shoes anywhere. Everything was quiet except for her sobbing. I got onto hands and knees and stood up when I could. The room swung and I put out a hand to stop it. The big Chinese-moon lamp went on and off to my pulse.

When I could turn around, I saw there was no one here. The ache of the rabbit-chop throbbed but I reached the bedroom still on my feet. She was crouched naked on the end of the bed and there was blood on her legs, so I went back and used the phone, dialing from the list she kept. He said he would come.

In the bedroom I put out the main lamps and knelt and took her face between my hands, and began worrying, nothing to do with her but to do with them, because they shouldn't have gone. Then I knew why they had gone. I said:

"There's a doctor on his way."

She nodded between my hands. She wouldn't let me touch her. She crouched with her legs tight together, rocking slowly.

"I have to leave you, Inga. If they come back it'll start again." She didn't say anything and I worried the thing out, and understood why she didn't ask me to stay. Later I would think clearly about this and set up the perspective. For the moment, all I could do was get the hang of the way things were going and act on impromptu understanding.

I wrote a number on a Kleenex from the dressing table and left it on the bed. "If you want to, after this, you can always get a message to me by phoning this number." I put a bathrobe around her shoulders and sat and held her until the doctor came.

He asked me what had happened to me, and I realized my face would be showing the aftereffects of the induced syncope and the rabbit-blow: film of sweat, bloodshot eyes, so forth. I told him it wasn't me, and showed him the bedroom before I left.

The street was bright. The innocent afternoon was ended, and it was night.

I was in time to fade in on Portuguese Canning.

Quota Freight was 132. Plus 3¼. *No report from you. Acknowledge and reassure. If corner system RT.*

Clucking like hens. I didn't like it. Through Hengel or Brand or some unemployed scout loafing in my field, they'd got wind of my clash with Phönix and wanted to know the score. They weren't worried about me. They were worried about my being caught and grilled successfully because I was now a hot operator and could blow the Bureau sky high if I were made to talk.

So now I was given homework to do. It filled three pages of paper with the name of the hotel cut off. Items included:

I don't think Rothstein was operating in liaison with anybody or working to any joint purpose. His own purpose was always, ultimately, to avenge his wife. The canister probably contains microfilm with a bang-destruction unit.

If Solly hadn't died in the way he did, I would have asked the Z Commission to open that canister because I was fairly certain the contents could have led me straight to Zossen. As things were, I didn't want anything to do with it.

Phönix is going to a lot of trouble with me and it seems reasonable to think that they have a great deal to keep in hush, and are very keen to find out how much I know. So far I know nothing.

This was just to needle them and I knew it but decided to let it stand. It was only five days since Pol had contacted me, and I had given myself a month for the mission. They had a nerve anyway, signaling me to report.

Don't quite understand your request for "reassurance" at this early stage. Have you been getting in the way of off-center info?

This was to tell them they could keep Hengel and Brand and anyone else out of my territory. Obviously somebody had reported my red sectors; it was even possible that the Bureau had a man doubling on the fringe and trying to find his way in, as I was myself; and he could have passed a report saying that I was in a corner. Well they could all bloody well shut up.

No justification for using RT.

RT didn't stand for radio-telephone but for Rabinda-Tanath, meaning the emergency system for phoning Local Berlin in that language. Had they clean forgotten what kind of thing a corner could be? There's never a telephone there.

I still hadn't got it off my chest so I ended:

Would respectfully suggest that unless there is definite info on my being in trouble, no unnecessary "reassurance" requests should be sent. If I am cornered I shall report accordingly. Q.

Time was now 9:07 and the depression was setting in because of the blood on her legs and the way Oktober had simply left the arena. It wasn't going to work and he didn't yet know that, so it would take him a short time to understand and alter his tactics—*unless* the doubling were perfect.

I am never happy when the adverse party gets confused because there's the interim period of correction and he is for this period like a bad bull that won't run straight, and you're closer to a high *cornada* than you'd ever be with an honest five-year-old Miura running on rails.

It took something like an hour to collate all the findings that stemmed from the events of the innocent afternoon, and to edit them and form detailed conclusions. General inference: starting out to hunt Zossen I'd been forced on the defensive twice within the first five days and hadn't learned more than half a dozen names that weren't already logged in the memorandum. The offensive would have to be taken as soon as possible, because once Oktober decided that I knew nothing *except* what his and Fabian's questions had implied, he would have me wiped out before I started getting solid facts and feeding them into Control.

One vital check had to be made before I chose my offensive position, and it had to be made now.

The distance was some three kilometers and the pavements were drying, so I left the BMW 1500 in the lock-up at the hotel and walked. Within five minutes I sensed a tag and led him northwest along the Hildburghauserstrasse at a slow pace because his presence had mentally thrown me and I wanted time to think. I hadn't expected him.

Findings: he must be flushed. I was reluctant to do this because he had his uses, but it was no go. What had happened was that no one had tagged me from the Grunewald Bridge until the beginning of the afternoon when I arrived at Inga's flat, because they'd known I could be picked up there. They hadn't known my new base: the Hotel Zentral. But they'd put a tag on wheels behind me when I had driven in the BMW from her flat in Wilmersdorf to the Zentral in Mariendorf—and I hadn't known it. It was simply that Oktober was taking no chances, and this was pleasing because it showed how worried he was.

They now knew my present base. This man had tagged me from there and was still at work. That was all right because there was absolutely no way of going over to the offensive without first showing Phönix my new base: to reach them I must first let them know where to reach me.

But I was committed to making this vital preliminary check, and it had to be done solo. Therefore he must be got rid of.

He was first class, and it took almost an hour. The whole business of tagging is one of the most routine and boring aspects of any operator's work. He can never walk down a street without making constant checks, especially if he is going somewhere strict hush, and he can burn up valuable time in having to flush the tag once he senses him. But if the game goes on long enough, it can be *impossible* to keep your tag on a man. In a city the size of Berlin, if he doesn't want you there, you'll eventually lose him. I have lost hundreds, and hundreds have lost me. In a few cases the boredom of well-worn tactics becomes overridden by the interplay of the game itself, and this is what now happened.

He was damned good and I had to take him through four hotels and twice through Lichterfelde-Süd station before I flushed him at the south end of the Berlinerstrasse and took up my original course.

Time was now 11:21 and the bar was closing. It was called the Brunnen and I had never been there before. The *Kellner* viewed me from between the chair-legs with his night-pallor face and thought out what phrase he would choose if I asked for a drink. There was only one other man in here, halfway up a stepladder winding the clock; he didn't even see me come or go.

I asked the *Kellner* the way to Südende station and went back into the street, making a whole series of rapid checks.

It was completely clear. I was alone. It was, in a way, a big moment in my life, and I savored it. The night air felt clean in my lungs and my shoes were springy on the empty pavement and for a few minutes I was aware of the remote possibility of the ultimate redemption of mankind. This modest turn of madness had the effect of a whiff of ammonia, clearing the head. It was a feeling that some operators may or may not experience once or twice in their careers. In actual speech it would go:

Here you are again in the thick of a job that you're doing because you choose to do it even though it may kill you around the next corner. It gets in the hair and the eyes and mouth and you never feel really clean, except for these few minutes, because you've just struck a blow that was bone on bone and it sent them reeling. Drink, brother, this may not come to you again.

My day ended in this way. It was midnight when I got back to the hotel. I fell asleep like an innocent man, with all those scars on the mind quieted as if by a balm. Tomorrow the offensive would be launched, at dawn when the streets would be empty.

16 | CIPHER

The dawn offensive was not spectacular, opening as it did with nothing more than a quiet stroll.

He was waiting for me when I left the Hotel Zentral. I didn't actually see him but I knew where he was. The street was residential but had a bar at the corner, some small distance from the hotel entrance. I knew he would be there. It was the only place. He would be somewhere behind the gray-white net curtains, watching for me.

To warm him up, I turned along the street in the other direction so that he had to get out of the bar and start his tag at a distance. He wouldn't like that. There was nothing moving in the street at this hour but myself, and the morning was windless. He must have tracked me over this first section with his fingers crossed hard: I had only to turn my head once to spot him. I didn't turn my head. We went north toward the center of the city where it would be more crowded.

The operation we were now engaged on was known as the switch. When an operator starts out to shadow another, the outcome will be found among five main possibilities. One: the tag is never noticed, and the shadowed man leads the adverse party to his destination, unknowing. (It seldom happens. An operator who doesn't even notice a tag isn't allowed to stay in the business very long.) Two: the tag is noticed but can't be flushed, in which case the operator must simply lead him a dance and leave his original destination unexposed. Three: the tag is noticed and then flushed, and the operator can then make for his original destination unaccompanied. Four: the tag is noticed, flushed, and challenged. (I did this with young Hengel. In that case my tag was not an adverse party, but it makes little difference: there's always a temptation to challenge after flushing, if only to see their face go red.) Five: the tag is noticed, flushed, *and followed.* The switch has been made, and the tag is now tagged.

We don't often do it, because an operator is never off-duty. He is always going somewhere and usually it's important that he gets there as soon as he can. On this occasion I used the switch because I had to go over to the offensive and find where the Phönix had its nest. It might be where I had been taken for the narcoanalysis session, but I was getting bored with being taken to places and followed to places (Inga's flat). The idea was to draw the enemy's fire so that we could come to grips, and I had done that successfully, but it was no good fetching a bellyful of Amytal whenever we closed together. I now had to find their base, go in under my own steam, get information on it, and then get clear with the skin on.

Two untapped sources of information were mine for the taking but I wasn't going to take them. Solly Rothstein's sealed container was one. Unless I were missing something, that container held all the vital information that he'd tried to bring me when they'd shot him down. It would lead me right to the Phönix base. I wanted to get there without trading on the death of a friend I'd helped to kill. Inga was the other untapped source. She was a defector of long standing but I would not trade on our innocent afternoon and ask her to give me all the information she had at the time of her defection. (This was how she would see things, and I must play it her way.)

The single route to their base was open to me: the tag who was behind me now must be made to lead me there. It was almost the only justification for a switch.

By nine o'clock I had managed to check him visually twice. He was a new man and less efficient than the one I'd flushed the night before. Forty-five minutes later I flushed him outside Kempinski's in the Kurfürstendamm, though clumsily. (He nearly got run over crossing the zebra on the red.) We spent half an hour dodging about and then he went into a phone-kiosk to report on the situation. His orders became obvious within ten minutes: he took a taxi and I followed him in mine, all the way back to the Hotel Zentral in Mariendorf. He had lost me, hadn't a hope of picking me up again by chance, and had been ordered back to our starting-point, the only known place where I could be found.

We were both annoyed. The morning was wasted. I had borne it in mind, when launching my damp-squib offensive, that he wouldn't *necessarily* lead me to his own base after I did the switch. It had been hope, not expectancy, that had started me off. There had been no other way of trying to get near their base again.

But tagging is like driving: an experienced operator does it automatically, and can think about other things while he's doing it. I had thought a lot about Solly Rothstein between Mariendorf and the Kurfürstendamm and back, and it had been brain-thinking. Before, it had been stomach-thinking, emotional thinking. Guilty because of his death, I'd let myself believe that to use the information inside that container would be to trade on tragedy, to exploit Solly for my own purposes. But my purposes were his. If I could kill off Phönix, a Nazi organization, it would avenge the murder of his wife; and Solly had lived for that and died for it.

I phoned Captain Stettner at the Z Bureau. He said:

"I've been trying to make contact with you. I didn't know where you'd moved."

There was no audible sign of line-tap but we didn't have to take chances so I just told him I would go to his office within the hour.

Sleet had started so I used the BMW, not even checking the mirror. They knew I was linked with the Z Polizei already. On the way I thought about Kenneth Lindsay Jones because the question of the Grunewaldsee had been coming up at me again, on and off. I thought I'd answered it: Oktober had told them to drop my corpse into the Grunewald because he knew I was listening and would be convinced that they were genuine orders to kill, since that was where KLJ was dumped. That answer might be correct but now I suspected it, simply because it kept on calling for my attention. It would have to be dealt with.

The only clue might lie in KLJ's last report to Control before he died. The information in that report was already filed in my head, taken from the burned memorandum; but I had never seen the report itself. If KLJ had had any premonition of his death it would be there in the phrasing of his report, and the memorandum didn't quote reports verbatim. It carried edited information only.

I signaled Control before reaching the Z Bureau, using a letter-card.

Request early sight of last KLJ report in original form. Hotel Zentral Mariendorf.

Captain Stettner was alone in his office and greeted me with slight embarrassment. He was a man typical of his stock, with a strong face and clear, unimaginative eyes. Let him follow a saint and he would do saintly things; put him to work with a devil and he would out-foul Satan. They are born to obey, these men, born to be led, and it's luck that elects their leader. Stettner was young, perhaps thirty, and so he was working for a liberal chancellor; it was his duty to bring in the henchmen of a long-dead maniac and to hand them to justice. Had he been fifteen years older he would have graduated from the Hitler Youth in 1939 to command an S.S. company pledged to genocide in the glorious name of the Führer.

He said to me: "You are not sleeping well, Herr Quiller."

"I haven't the time." It wasn't lack of sleep that was showing in my face, but the strain of Oktober's succession of treatments. It irked me that it showed. "You said you were trying to contact me?"

"Yes. I'm sorry you didn't feel it necessary to give me your change of address."

"I didn't know you'd need my help."

His embarrassed air increased. "I assume our relationship to be one of mutual assistance."

No answer. I studied the clearness of his skin and the freshness of his eyes and wished I were thirty, so that whatever I went through it didn't show in my face.

"I believe you knew Dr. Solomon Rothstein well?" he asked me suddenly.

"I knew him a long time ago."

"In the war?"

"Yes."

"Would you tell me what kind of work he was doing, in the war?"

I said: "In what precise way can I mutually assist you, Herr Stettner?"

"Of course you are not obliged to answer my questions, Herr Quiller—"

"That's right. You talk, and I'll listen."

He considered this and I could see the brightly polished cogs going round inside his transparent plastic skull. He worked for the Federal Government. I worked for an intelligence service of an Occupying Power, and was therefore of a technically higher status. Therefore I called the tune. When he got it set out correctly, he followed procedure and said unemotionally:

"We have been trying to break a cipher and we have so far failed. I hoped you might succeed, since you once worked with Dr. Rothstein and might remember any cipher systems he used."

I knew what had happened.

"We can't trace his brother in Argentina—Isaac Rothstein. We have now opened the canister that was found in the laboratory on the Potsdamerstrasse, after checking it for explosives with magnetic sounding. It contains a glass phial and a sheet of paper covered with cipher."

It was some time since I'd had a piece of luck. I had expected a lot of trouble in persuading them to open the container and even more trouble in persuading them to show me what was inside.

I said: "I'll have a go."

He tried not to look relieved. "We are keeping the original, and will give you an exact copy. It's unnecessary to warn you that it must not be let out of your close possession."

"I thought of offering the publication rights to *Der Spiegel*."

He spun in his chair. "But that would be *unthinkable*, Herr Quiller! Surely you must realize that the very highest possible secrecy has to be . . . maintained . . ." And the wind went out of him slowly while I watched him. A wan smile came to his face. "Of course . . . a little joke. Of course."

He took time to recover. I asked him: "Are you thinking of opening the glass phial?"

"My superiors believe it might be very dangerous to do that. Dr. Rothstein's main work was carried out in a special laboratory behind the one that was raided, and it is sealed off with decontamination airlocks. One of his staff has been interrogated and has warned us that Dr. Rothstein was researching certain strains of bacteria highly dangerous to man. Unless the ciphered material specifies any good reason for our opening the glass phial it will probably be put into a furnace, still sealed." He gave me a plain gray envelope. "This is your copy, Herr Quiller. May I wish you success."

On the way to Mariendorf, a small gray NSU became lodged in the driving-mirror and I led it to within a kilometer of the Hotel Zentral. I wasn't going there but I went in that direction to give the impression that I was, so that the flush would be easier: anticipating my destination, though wrongly, the tag would be unprepared for a sudden change of route. I lost him in a turning off the Rixdorfstrasse and got clear, heading for the park and running the BMW into a gap between two other cars that stood empty outside the lodge.

The decipherment might take several days. If I sat like a duck at the Hotel Zentral working on it, they could come for me whenever they liked, and I didn't want to see Oktober again until I was ready. He wouldn't wait long. I knew why he'd left Inga's flat, and it wasn't because he thought he could never get me to talk. He would go on trying until one of the higher executives gave the order to kill me off as useless. Since leaving the flat last night, I had been under constant observation and they'd now be worried about the two flushes of today.

If they came for me at the hotel and caught me with the Rothstein document they'd haul me in and keep me held until they'd tried to break the cipher, and if they failed they would try to break me. The Hotel Zentral was a permanent red sector now.

The park was deserted. Sleet hit the windows of the car and slid down in rivulets. The engine was still warm so I turned on the heater fan and worked up a fug.

The single sheet was copied in typed capitals. I took a letter-card and drew the skeleton boxing. The pale afternoon light threw water-patterns from the windows across the paper, and it seemed to be melting as I studied it.

First considerations: was this code, cipher, or an unfamiliar language? Three or four of the words indicated a cipher; two of them comprised solely the letter N and there was more than one instance of a word comprising double A. This wouldn't happen with a code, and it was unlikely that even a lost language of Asia or South America would have a double vowel as a complete word. There was a thousand-to-one risk of my spending days on this task without realizing I was trying to decipher the indecipherable: a purely unknown language.

Darmba valthala-mah im jhuma, for example, is pure Rabinda-Tanath and means "fire-cart kills very quick." I had put this into speech for Fabian the narcoanalyst and he'd imagined it to be gibberish *or* a foreign tongue. In writing it would still look like gibberish, *or* like a foreign language, *or* like a cipher. To propose an absurd case: anyone who had never heard or seen French might take the word *arbre* for cipher, and if he assumed A = M, R = O, B = T, E = R, he would finish up with the word *motor*. Obviously he wouldn't get far because he would soon find that most of the other words were turned into gibberish by applying the same assumption. (*Barre* would give *tmoor*, which is meaningless.) But he could waste hours of time trying different assumptions (A = B, C, D, etc.) before he realized he was dealing with the indecipherable: a foreign language.

But the N and the double A ruled out the chance that Solly had written this document in a little-known tongue with which his brother was familiar.

Assumption: cipher. Stettner's cryptographers agreed with this.

All ciphers are broken by applying three tools: mathematics, the laws of frequency, and trial-and-error. The most experienced cryptographer uses these three tools and plies them with patience, the prime mover.

I was not experienced. Two months at the training school and the infrequent sight of cryptograms during a mission was all I knew of the business, and normally I would shoot this document straight over to Control for their own team of specialists to break. But there might be something in Captain Stettner's idea: my knowledge of Solly Rothstein could provide a key. (In the same terms, the original report sent in by KLJ could give me clues to his death and its circumstances, where the edited and depersonalized information could not.)

The sheet on my knees carried twenty-five lines averaging ten words to the line. First checks on frequency gave the use of the letter K one hundred and thirty times. Possible E. The number of L's was ninety-seven. Possible T. The X's numbered sixty-one. Possible A. So on.

Check a cipher word, XELK. Gave A-TE. ANTE was the only possibility. No go. *Anti* would have given more hope, since it was a suffix used in most sciences, biology included (antibiotic), but even then it wouldn't stand alone. I went on to double letters in terms of frequency: LL, EE, SS, so on, thinking in English and German. Tried combinations: TH, HE, AN, so on. Treble-combination frequencies: THE, ING, AND, ION, ENT, so on. Back-checked and amalgamated with singles, doubles, trebles, English and German.

One interesting point was that there was no equal grouping to avoid a single letter standing alone. This is often done to avoid leaving blatant clues: a single letter standing alone is almost certain to be A or I. Two letters standing alone would be IN, ON, AN, so on. Therefore, I SHALL SEND IN A REPORT would be grouped in batches of five, using one "null" at the end of the final group as a filler: ISHAL LSEND INARE PORTW. The ciphering would follow. But the groups here were unequal, with words comprising single, double, and treble letters. These could be themselves "nulls" peppered at random to confuse the pattern.

Five words were composed of fifteen letters or more, but this was to be expected: they were probably the Latin names of bacilli. I left them out of my present reckoning.

Trial and error. Apply singles, doubles, trebles, try the same again: reverse and read backward, add prefix and suffix nulls, assume *all* singles and doubles to be nulls . . .

The sleet hit the windows softly.

Solly, what is it you want so urgently to tell your brother?

ELFTE—PSKLIO—JZFDX—LWO . . . No go, no go.

The afternoon light was fading. Steam was thick inside the windows, and I turned off the heater.

Solly, what did you put in your little glass phial? For good or for evil, and for whom?

SLK. FPQC. OS. SPRIT. *Sprit!* German. Alcohol. Alcohol used in biological research. Check it. ASSWZ. No go . . . a false alarm. (But there's nothing like it to spur you on, an occasional promise of success, however false.)

When it was too dark to see the words without putting a light on, I got out of the car and locked it, walking for an hour through the raw half-dark of the streets to circulate the blood and take on oxygen; then I did a further four and a half hours' stint without moving the BMW, and finished where I had begun, with not one single word deciphered. But the groundwork was almost over. The document was written in one of sixteen thousand two hundred and twenty ciphers, and I still had to find out which; but it couldn't be found by going through the lot (a task of approximately twenty-one months, working eight hours per day and six days per week with no vacations), and there were ways in that must be found and taken.

At ten o'clock a *Schnitzel* and some *Moselwein*, and the thought of home and bed. Unattractive. Home was the place where they might come for me at any minute, but if I left the Hotel Zentral it would worry Oktober. It must be shown that I was ready to hold myself available, placing my trust in the situation of his own devising. For another day—but no longer than that—he could be allowed to think that his present plan would work. After that, I would have to change it and pursue my own.

I had chosen a restaurant of cheap aspect, where the lavatory could be expected to have a certain amount of warped woodwork somewhere instead of elegant tiling throughout. If the choice was wrong, it would mean finishing the evening at a bar with an Apollinaris; as it was, there was a partition of flimsy timber here at the restaurant and the document was folded thrice and slipped between two joists where it would be safe for the night. Then I went home.

The BMW was run into the lock-up and the key taken upstairs. A five-minute check assured me that my room had been neither searched nor rigged with booby traps or a mike. Half a minute to reach a brain-think decision to override the stomach-think wish to telephone the Brunnen Bar, the number of which I had written on the Kleenex for Inga. Sleep, with a swarm of typed capitals plaguing my dreams.

It was noon next day when I took out the car and checked the tag in the mirror within a kilometer of the hotel. It was different again: a metalescent Taunus 12M that dogged me through two ambers before closing up and flicking its lights on and off. I chose the same park where I had worked all through the afternoon and evening of yesterday, and stopped the car near the lodge. The Taunus pulled up behind and I got out before he did, just in case, and stood waiting for him.

17 | FERRET

We were alone in the silent park. The winter-day light fell on us as we faced each other. He stood still, letting me remember his features. A round face with mud-brown eyes unmagnified by the plain lenses of his schoolboy-type glasses. A black velour hat, that I hadn't seen on him the first time. I was satisfied.

"All I wanted was the report," I told him. "They could have sent anyone. Hengel or someone."

"They sent me to talk to you. I would have contacted you two days ago but you didn't tell us you'd moved to the Zentral." I remembered the Rhenish accent. He asked: "Why aren't they tagging you?"

He had taken note that no other car but his own had dogged me from the hotel just now.

"I'm on ice."

"No observation at all?"

"They've got a man at the bar opposite, or they did have, yesterday." I had been puzzled, myself, at the absence of a tag when I'd driven from the hotel that morning. I never liked being given too much rope, for the classic reason.

"We are getting worried about you," he said.

He meant worried about my being made to talk. "They won't break me," I told him.

"They've tried."

I wondered how much he knew. Control always knew more about an operator than he thought. I know when I'm being followed but I don't always know when I'm being observed, and they might have posted Hengel or Brand or any of their scouts to watch the Hotel Prinz Johann. As soon as they had received my signal requesting the KLJ report they might have posted a man on the Zentral.

The idea annoyed me and I tested him. "July, August, September."

The light flickered across his glasses as he nodded. "Yes, we know about Oktober."

"For how long?"

"Seven months."

Before my time, and even before Kenneth Lindsay Jones's. Charington had been operating on this mission, seven months ago. It was probably Oktober who had killed him. It was probably Oktober who had killed Jones. Now Control was worried about me.

Our breath steamed on the air. I said:

"All I wanted was the report."

"I have brought it."

"Don't give it to me now."

"Of course not."

The park looked deserted, a ring of trees phantom-gray in the winter air. We could both be wrong: there *might* have been a tag following both our cars from the Zentral. He might be among those trees. If Pol were seen to pass anything to me, they would be after it very fast.

He said in his modulated tone: "I was sent to bring you the report and to brief you. We know less than you do about Oktober and Phönix, but we know more about the general background than you. The overall picture."

"Control doesn't have to tell me any more than it thinks I have to know—"

"Don't misunderstand me. I was briefed to give you the whole background the first time I contacted you, but you weren't ready to be convinced, so I didn't persist. You didn't think the German General Staff might be prepared to launch any kind of armed operation, given the means and the chance."

"I still don't."

"Then what do you think your mission is?"

"I'm just an operator sent into the opposite warren like a ferret. That's all right, it's what I'm for, it's what I like doing. But if I finally pick off Zossen and Oktober and the top echelon of the whole Phönix organization, I don't think I shall have done any more than blow down a pack of cards. I don't think the German General Staff knows anything about Phönix, or is interested, any more than the British War Office is interested in mods and rockers."

He was a man of peculiar patience. He would have made a good schoolteacher. He waited for a few seconds so that I had time to replay the echoes of my own voice, and he got results. I was right, I was a ferret in a warren, but I was also wrong: a ferret couldn't expect to know anything at all about the German General Staff or what it was doing or what it was thinking. Control knew more than I. It always does. That's why we kick up rough, perhaps, when we can't see the sense of its policy.

When he had given me my few seconds to think, he said quietly: "If you help us to bring down Phönix, you'll save a million lives and it will almost certainly cost you yours. We know this. We know this." His mud-brown eyes stared at me without blinking. "If you underestimate what you are doing, you won't do it well. We want the best from you, the very best, while you have the time left to give it."

The air was clammy against my face. The ring of trees was cemetery-quiet.

"That is why we are worried about you," his calm voice said. "We want you to take this mission seriously. If you let yourself imagine we have sent you into this particular search area on a routine mission to get information and nothing more, you won't work at your best. We *do* want information, badly. We want to know where Phönix has its base. *They* want information, too, and as badly. They want to know how much *we* know of their intentions. Their most direct way of getting that information is through you."

I decided to let him go on talking. He was perfectly correct about this. Oktober was handling me as no adverse party had ever tried to handle me before. His two attempts to break me—by narcoanalysis and then torture at one remove—followed a normal pattern; but he was giving me rope by the mile at every other stage. I had run right across their line of fire when Solly was killed; they had walked out on me after the scene at Inga's flat; they had let me go to see Captain Stettner yesterday. A dozen times, at the Prinz Johann and at the Zentral and in the open at a dozen places, they could have hauled me in and broken me up physically at their leisure in the hope of getting information on how much Control knew of Phönix. But the more rope I took, the more they gave me.

Probably they hadn't got enough out of Charington so they killed him off before he got too much out of them. The same with KLJ. They were giving me a longer run, concentrating on me instead of relying on their own agents to crack open Control itself.

"We are worried," Pol said, "that you don't understand your position. It is this. There are two opposing armies drawn up on the field, each ready to launch the big attack. But there is a heavy fog and they can't sight each other. You are in the gap between them. You can see us, but so far you can't see them. Your mission is to get near enough to see them, and signal their position to us, giving us the advantage. That is where you are, Quiller. In the gap."

He waited again so that I could consider.

All he hadn't said was that once I got near enough to Phönix to give that signal, my part would be played and I would become expendable, would *have* to be expendable, because the chances of surviving were slight.

Well, I would get near to them, and I would send the signal, and I would bloody well survive.

But the ring of trees was so quiet, a ring of tombstones.

I said: "All I want is the report. Then stop getting in my way."

I walked back to the BMW and sat inside. He leaned through the window so that his body covered it, and dropped the envelope onto the seat beside me. His face was dark in the gloom of the interior.

"Never forget," he said, "that the whole of our organization is behind you, at every minute."

"Just keep it clear of me."

I read the last testament. The writing was thin and hurried.

Dec. 3. Tags now a nuisance, time wasted in flushing. But have got a line on base, will confirm soon. Things very tricky now, request no contacts any account. May not receive Bourse. May not signal for a time. KLJ.

The restaurant was full and I sat working on the report, fiddling with an underdone lump of *Schweinefleisch*.

So he had reached much the same stage as I had reached now, and had told them—as I had told Pol an hour ago—*keep clear of me*. Then he had gone in, right the way in, and couldn't be allowed to live.

A line on base. What line? It didn't matter. He had followed it and they had killed him off because he was too close. So here was the address of the Phönix base. I had been there myself without being allowed to know where it was. Now I knew where it was.

I put the slip of paper back into the envelope, which was already addressed to Eurosound. The man brought my bill and I paid it, going to the lavatory and using a penknife to ease out the Rothstein document. There was a post-box at the intersection not far from the restaurant and I sent off the report as promised. One quick turn round the block showed there was no foot-tag, but I had been followed to the restaurant by the small gray NSU, because I had called at the Zentral after leaving Pol and they'd picked me up from there. It was parked five cars behind my BMW. I didn't want to waste time flushing him and I didn't want to risk being snatched with the document on me. There was a *Polizei* officer on duty at the intersection, so I crossed over and showed him the Z Commission *Ausweis* that Captain Stettner had given me: it was no more than a *laisser-passer* into the Z Bureau backroom departments, but it would probably do.

I said: "I've reason to believe that there's a man in a stolen car across the road. The NSU number BN.LM.11, outside the *Friseur*. You may care to check it."

We walked together to the other side and I hung back as we passed my BMW. He didn't miss me because he was sizing up the NSU as he approached it, and as I drove away I saw him in the mirror, checking the driver's papers.

It took half an hour to change the BMW at the Hertz office but it would have taken longer than that to flush the tag and I had now altered the image. I couldn't risk being picked up by sheer chance from now on, because I had the document on me and because, as KLJ had put it, things were very tricky now.

A million lives, Pol had said. And mine. A million and one. Because I was going to survive. The man in London wasn't going to light another cigarette and send for a replacement.

I had never whistled in the dark before and the tune came thinly.

The new image was a very fast 230 SL pagoda-top Mercedes with fuel-injection, the last thing they would look for, and I took it right out west to the edge of the Havel and parked on the Schildhorn peninsula. Mist shrouded the waterscape and the light was gray. The monument poked its sandstone finger at the sky, and I didn't look at it more than once because everything reminded me of cemeteries.

Treble-combination frequencies in English and German: ING—ENT—SCH—EUN. Check and assume, re-check. No go.

Two hours by the black-and-gold clock on the fascia, cramp in the legs.

Reverse and read backward, add prefix and suffix nulls: LKA-OEI—JUQOP—AJSHGFRWEQT. Pick a new set and stay clear of the multisyllabics, obviously Latin for bugs.

Four hours and the circulation seizing up.

A walk by the beautiful waterside, dead land and dead water, a mezzotint laced with the somber dark of the pines, a place for lost souls and ferrets, with the sirensong crying softly across the mirrored sky: "AJSHGFRWEQT!" they sang. "OQUISTRI!"

The only living thing I saw the whole of the afternoon was a dog that came from the mist and pissed at the foot of the monument and vanished as it had come.

Patience.

Possible key: U = S, B = M, O = A, eight others. Pick a long one for pride's sake: VASOSFGWOBU. Gave OTNANGILAMS. Reverse and add prefix and suffix nulls. Gave SMALIGNANTO.

Nearly missed it because it sounded Spanish.

Drop prefix and suffix nulls. MALIGNANT.

Check another. Thought we had *Sprit*, German for alcohol, yesterday. But hope has a grasshopper leap.

RCIMEDIPEF. Drop nulls and reverse: EPIDEMIC.

Come in, Solly, come in . . .

18 | OBJECT 73

The hands of Captain Stettner had begun shaking. The paper he was holding almost fluttered.

I sat facing him, trying to think, but gave it up. The room was so filled with his horror that detached thought was impossible. He picked up a telephone long before he had finished reading my deciphered version of the Rothstein document.

"Fifteen," he said to the switchboard.

That would be their forensic laboratory, the safest place for keeping a glass phial whose contents might be dangerous.

"Captain Stettner," he said, his voice only just under control. "You have an object numbered 73 in your keeping. Have you received any orders to open it?" He went on staring at me, and I remembered his uneasiness when the bogus doctor from Phönix had come to this office to inject him. "Then if you receive any such order, refer to me first, immediately. I have information that the contents are highly dangerous. Please take all steps to insure that it remains sealed and locked away. Accidental breakage could cause a whole-scale disaster."

He went on a bit more about this, and there was a mist of sweat on the receiver when he put it down. Then I had to wait while he finished reading the decipherment. The single sheet of paper went on fluttering in his hands.

"I don't know," he said at last, "anything about these matters.

Anything about this bacillus. Do you?" He was like a child pleading to be comforted, to be told that it wasn't really dark, only nighttime.

"Not much," I said.

He was running the back of his hand around his face. "I mean," he asked without hope, "is it possible that Dr. Rothstein was deranged in some way?"

"In a world as mad as this, how do we define derangement?"

No comfort in that. He tried again. "This—this talk of a *plague* . . . Could one small phial cause such a thing?"

I wished he'd straighten up so that I could sound him on the general background of Solly's operations. Perhaps it would be quicker in the long run to tell him the worst and then put a few questions of the kind that interested me more.

"Yes, a phial that size could do it. At this moment, America, Russia, England, France, Japan, and China—there are probably others—are researching on *botulinus* toxin, culturing it and killing it to provide the basis for an antidote. Eight ounces of it could wipe out the world population. We all need the antidote, just as we all need the best anti-missile missile, to make sure we can go on living in brotherly love. It may be that Rothstein was also working on that toxin, but it isn't what he put into the phial. That's just one of the plague-group."

A telephone began ringing and he cut the switch, so I carried on. "There are three forms of plague. The classic bubonic type causes the superficial lymph glands to swell and suppurate into dark abscesses. Type two, the septicemic, poisons the blood. Type three affects the lung. It's even more infectious than the bubonic, which killed off a quarter of the population of Europe in the fourteenth century—the English called it the Black Death. This third type is the pneumonic. Dr. Rothstein gives it the more correct name in that document: *Pasteurella pestis*. It's a rod-shaped bacillus that can be grown in a laboratory on suitable culture medium. Once it gets loose, infection is by exhaled droplets and the incubation period is a short one: three or four days. Three times quicker than smallpox."

He didn't look comforted. He said dully: "A quarter of the population of Europe. Did you say that?"

"At that time, twenty-five million people." My thoughts ran on aloud, just as they had at the Nürnberg Trial when I had spoken of Heinrich Zossen. "A heavy toll of human life, *mein Hauptmann*, I agree. Even the Nazi plague of our own century wiped out only half that number in the death camps."

It didn't register. He was thinking of Argentina, and object number 73. I tied the ends for him: "Natural resistance to the pneumonic plague in South America is fairly low at present because there hasn't been an epidemic there for a long time, though it's *en*demic in Brazil, Peru, and Ecuador. So I would say that if Dr. Rothstein's brother in Argentina had opened that phial and tipped the contents from the balcony of a packed cinema, as instructed, the seventy thousand Germans and ex-Nazis in San Caterina would be dead within a week."

He said nothing for a full fifteen seconds.

"Herr Quiller . . . Why did he want to do this?"

"Because they killed his wife."

"But I do not understand. It is one of your little jokes, again."

"I hope you'll never understand. You're too young to understand. You must ask your elders. They know about these things. They killed twelve million people in five years. Half were Jews. And you can hear their reason for killing six million *Judenfrei* when you listen to them pleading their innocence at the courts. They say they killed them because they were 'only Jews.' Nothing personal, you see. No hate, or thoughts of vengeance, or even fear. Just the Yellow Star, the selection camp, and the gas chamber. Difficult to understand. But I understand Dr. Rothstein's reason better. He was committed to personal vengeance and it was measured solely by the depths of his love for one woman and by the desolation of her loss to him. *And a thousand shall fall.*"

He got up and stood over me, a thin young man still trying to get to grips with the world he'd been born in.

"But the others! The plague wouldn't have stopped at any frontier. The whole of San Caterina—and then the whole of Argentina—"

"And beyond, until they got the diagnosis correct and put the sulpha drugs to work. Rough justice is like that: it takes the innocent as well. He knew that. He knew there are half a million of his own race in Argentina, but even *that* didn't stop him preparing that phial and writing this bequest to his brother. Dr. Rothstein meant to avenge his wife before he died, and if that wasn't possible he meant his death to bring it about."

Stettner looked down at me with his clear blue unimaginative eyes, and I was impatient with him because I'd just asked two of my questions about Solly's operational background and he didn't even catch on. Either that, or he didn't know anything more about Solly than I knew.

The day had gone badly for me and frustration was setting in. After two days' grinding work on the cipher, I had produced nothing that would take me any nearer to Phönix. This document could have nothing to do with what Solly had wanted to tell me. He wouldn't have any reason to tell me that his living obsession was to wipe out a South American town, because I couldn't be expected to champion the idea. Either his obsession had followed a normal course, pushing him across the edge of reason so that he was self-blinded to the risk of annihilating a whole continent, or he had made elaborate plans for his brother to organize an underground inoculation-scheme to save the innocent before the plague was set on the march. It made no difference to me or to my mission. If Isaac Rothstein were a sane man, he would have put the phial straight into an incinerator, realizing his brother's state of mind.

Solly would never have told me of this. Then what had he been so desperate to tell me? There was no clue in the document, which was simply a detailed form of instruction to his brother: how the bacillus was to be disseminated, how to avoid infection during the act of dissemination, steps to be taken during the four-day incubation period, so forth.

There was of course an obvious parallel to be assumed, and it would have to be thought about later when I had left the aura of Captain Stettner's pathological horror of disease.

Because I knew that Solly had been doubling.

"I am grateful to you, Herr Quiller," Stettner was saying. "I shall of course take this decipherment straight to my superiors."

Before I went I asked him: "Did you find anything else in that laboratory, anything significant, anything you decided not to tell me about?"

He seemed surprised. "Nothing."

"I've done you a service, Herr Hauptmann, and you would be the first to reciprocate. So I'll take your word that the canister was all you found."

"You have my word. Apart, of course, from the various papers we allowed you to see at the time. There was nothing else."

He wasn't lying. I wished he had been. It would have been something to bite on.

I left him and found the 230 SL where I had parked it, half a kilometer from the Z Bureau. It was a model they'd never expect to find me driving, but once they'd got onto it they'd tag me at a distance because it was so distinctive, and distance-tagging was difficult to sense. They knew I might visit the Z Bureau at any time, so the car had been parked well clear. But I was expecting a tag to show up and there wasn't one. The half-kilometer was a dead clear run and I got into the car with a sense of foreboding. The rope they were giving me was getting longer, and I feared it.

Going over to the offensive was more difficult than I'd thought. Two days wasted on the Rothstein document, with still no clue to the way in.

There was only one feature of the day's work that eased my frustration: I now believed in Pol and in his briefing. The German General Staff *did* have—or *might* have—the means of triggering a non-nuclear war. Because of the parallel assumption.

Night was down and the streets were shining with the aftermath of the sleet. There was a chance of getting the Mercedes into the

Hotel Zentral lock-up without being recognized. If they still had a man posted in the bar at the corner he would be watching for the BMW.

I waited on the far side of the traffic lights until a line of cars had built up, then followed the two who peeled off and took my street, keeping close behind them on the principle that one of three cars is less noticeable than a car traveling alone. The windows of the bar were steamed up, but there was a black area low down in one corner and I turned my head away as I passed the place, swinging into the glass-roofed courtyard of the hotel with the riding lights switched off.

The courtyard was oblong and the glass roof ran from the hotel building to the row of lock-ups. Observation could be kept on it only from the windows of the hotel itself and from a single house on the other side of the street, whose windows faced the open gates of the court. Three of these were lit and the fourth heavily curtained. The lower windows of the hotel were of frosted glass and the five upper ones were all lit. I hadn't been seen putting the new image into the lock-up, though I might have been seen driving it into the court.

Findings: the 230 SL was *probably* a good bet if I had to get away in a hurry.

Routine checks made on entering my room indicated no interference. They were keeping their distance, paying out the rope.

One hour's thought cleared up a lot of unanswered questions and posed some new ones. The Rothstein parallel assumption was given a thorough examination and still stood up. The frustration was eased a little and I even had the grace to send in a brief report to Control:

Correction to Signal 5. Container found at Rothstein lab didn't carry microfilm but a phial charged with heavy culture of pneumonic plague bacillus and ciphered message to R.'s brother in Argentina detailing method of starting epidemic in San Caterina. Contact Captain Stettner Z Bureau if want details.

Ten minutes with the feet above head-level, the eyes closed to shut out the faint lilac trellis-pattern wallpaper. Review mental hooks for the day. One left: telephone the Brunnen Bar.

The line was clear of tapping. There was indeed a message for Herr Quiller: would I please ring Wilmersdorf 38.39.01 before midnight?

She answered after the second ring. There was no tapping at her end either.

I asked: "Are you feeling better?" There had been blood on her thighs.

"I am better now."

"They gave me your message—"

"Yes. You must come to see me."

"Too dangerous, Inga. It could start all over again."

"There is no danger. You must come as soon as you can. I have something important for you. Believe me."

There was a choice of two reactions: to follow her view of the situation, or to follow mine. I said:

"I'll be with you in fifteen minutes."

My view of the situation might not be right but it was riskable. But I left the car in the lock-up, walking to the post-box and sending the signal before I got a taxi. I wanted the very fast 230 SL to stay unseen in case there was trouble and I had to drive myself out of it.

There was no apparent observation on the entrance to the block of apartments. The hall, lift, and top floor passage were deserted. I pressed the bell.

She was in a tunic and slacks of a red so vivid that it glowed on my hand as I touched her and burned in her eyes as she watched me. It was the first time I had seen her in color.

She said: "This is Helmut Braun."

He was a small soft-eyed man with slightly hooded lids and a short kittenish nose. He never put his hands anywhere but let them hang by his sides, and he was as confident as she was nervous. She glanced twice at the ebony table within the first half minute.

"I am officially working for them," he said to me with a shy smile.

I was on the wrong foot and the thought was unpleasant. We always try to estimate whatever situation we go into, beforehand— even a few seconds beforehand. It was twenty minutes since I had telephoned her and I was still unprepared for three things: the vivid red of her clothes, the presence of the man Braun, and the object lying on the table. It was a black-covered file of papers.

It would have to be played by ear, and we never like that.

"For them?" I asked him. He might be anyone, Z Commission, a doubler, one of her lovers. He wasn't in my group: there hadn't been a single "c" in his first sentence, nor "Windsor."

"Phönix." He smiled.

We were obviously here for business because he picked up the file and offered it to me with a pert bow. "This is for you, Herr Quiller."

Inga sat on the black Skai settee, a flame on charcoal. I looked at her once before I opened the file, but she was staring at her hands. The file was thin quarto and there was one word on the first sheet: *Sprungbrett*. Springboard.

I asked: "Do you want me to look at it right away?"

"We think you should." His accent was Bavarian.

They both watched my face as I turned the sheets. The second sheet carried a list of names, all of them high-ranking officers of the German General Staff. Next was a list of armed units on readiness. There followed the main outline of the operation, detailing preliminaries, major attack sectors, and spearheads. The operation was to be launched by carefully integrated land, sea, and air contingents immediately following a false announcement by five international news services that a bomb test in the Sahara had misfired and was spreading fallout across the Mediterranean. Under cover of alarm conditions, the immediate assaults would be directed against Gibraltar, Algeria, Libya, Israel, Greece, Cyprus, and Sicily. Franco in the west, Nasser in the east, and Mafia battalions taking hold in southern Italy. A *fait accompli* before the major powers could put out the fire. And this was only the springboard to a nonnuclear war in a nuclear age, with neither Russia nor the United States threatened.

It took me fifteen minutes to read the file, during which time no one spoke. I dropped it back onto the table and said:

"There's no date. No D-Day, no H-Hour."

Helmut Braun looked pained. "I hadn't noticed that. It would be very difficult for me to find out the date of the operation. It was highly dangerous for me in any case to get this file."

Inga had been watching me but now she looked at her hands again. I could tell nothing from her expression except that she was nervous about the whole thing. Braun was still looking hurt.

"There's a testing team set up in the Sahara," I said reflectively, "at the moment. No one's been told when they intend to fire their bomb."

"We can assume it is a matter of days, Herr Quiller."

I stood close to him and asked: "Why did you make it your business to get hold of this file and what decided you to let me see it?"

His hands hung at his sides. He looked at me straight in the eyes. "I am a friend of Inga's. She knows I am working against Phönix. She told me about you. I wanted to do something active—*definitive*—and it was a chance for me after so many years of passive opposition to them. Herr Quiller, I am a Jew." His hands moved at last, their fingers opening in an appeal for my understanding. "I can do nothing with this file, but you can. So I brought it to you."

Then Inga moved and hissed out a breath and he swung his eyes to her and then to the door. In silence he went across the room and bent at the door, listening.

Sixty seconds is a long time. The silence went on for longer than that, and he stood crouched like a cat at the door. She was beside me but I didn't look at her. Knowing that if there came another sound he would hear it, I left the situation in his hands and used the time for thinking.

It sometimes comes to people like us that we are faced with the terrible temptation of risking all on a single throw. This happened to me now. But we never throw blind. There have to be certainties in support of the decision to take a risk that size. In my case there were these:

I knew why the Brunnen Bar hadn't been put under observation on the night when Oktober had been here. I knew why Solly had been killed. I knew why Inga, tonight, was wearing red. And I knew why the briefing-draft of Operation Springboard had been given freely into my hands.

But certainties can lodge in the mind as a partial result of stomach-thinking, which is always dangerous. Sometimes the facts in our possession interlock so elegantly that we reject the few pieces that spoil the edge of the picture. Therefore a risk is always present when the all-or-nothing type of throw is made; but the risk is calculated.

Braun moved, coming away from the door.

"I am an easily frightened man," he said. "I wish I weren't like that. My operations would then be less passive, less ineffectual." He had spoken in a whisper.

I looked down at the file. "You're not doing badly."

It seemed to cheer him up and he asked: "You'll take it to your people?"

"Yes. As soon as I've got confirmation on it. My people like us to check this kind of thing at source, to save wasting time. And time looks short, with this one."

"How will you get confirmation?"

"I'll go to the source. The Phönix base. I know where it is. The house by the Grunewald Bridge."

At the edge of my field of vision I saw Inga begin shivering.

19 | THE SEPULCHER

He said: "You would never get out alive."

Inga was still shivering.

I picked up the file and he lifted his hand at once, saying, "I beg you not to go. But if you go, I beg you not to take the file with you."

"Don't worry, I won't say where I got it."

"You don't understand my position, Herr Quiller. They'll start an immediate inquiry at the highest level to find out who stole the file. They'll examine it for fingerprints, and mine are on it—so are Inga's." He held his hands limply. "Please," he said.

"All right." The file hit the table with a slap. "But you'll make it available to me when I get back?"

He sighed. "You will not get back." He looked at Inga for help, but she turned away and in a minute she came back with a coat on, a military-style trencher buttoning at the right. With her bright helmet of hair and the martial coat she looked all the things she was: man, woman, hermaphrodite, transvestite, a Joan of Arc. She said: "I'll go with you."

Braun closed his eyes. "Inga . . ." he said hopelessly.

He was standing like that when we went into the passage together. A man was closing the door of the lift but saw us coming and waited so that we could go down with him. We let him make his way ahead of us through the hall as a return of courtesy. Our footsteps echoed; the place was mostly marble, and sounds carried.

We turned along the pavement and there were steps behind us. It was Braun, trotting to catch up. "Herr Quiller," he said plaintively. "Inga . . ." We didn't say anything, so he gave it up, signaling a taxi from the rank and getting in with us.

The night was cold and clear and I watched the city as we passed along its streets. People were about, and the lights burned brilliantly as if they had never gone out nor would ever go out again; but not far away, where the Wall stood, I had often seen rabbits bobbing among the rubble of no man's land, in and out of the tank-traps and barbed wire and the shadows of the machine gun posts. In London you would see Piccadilly on one side, Leicester Square on the other, and in between a tract so desolate that rabbits ran there, safe from man.

I had told the driver: "Grunewaldbrück."

The house was there. The address was in the last report from Kenneth Lindsay Jones. He'd been closing in on the enemy, with "a line on base." Things were "very tricky" and he had warned Control that he "might not signal for a time" or even "receive Bourse." He had followed that line and they'd killed him off before he got too close to their base. They had shot him and dropped his body into the Grunewaldsee: *the nearest place*. It was from the Grunewald Bridge that they had dropped me, into that same water.

We were going there now, to the house by the bridge with the single plantain tree outside, the tree I had seen through the window when I had sat trapped in the silk brocade chair.

The glint of water under starlight was now on our left, and I began counting the streets on the other side, with the Verderstrasse as a reference. Then suddenly Braun shifted forward and told the driver to pull up.

"I will not go in with you," he told us. "I would die of fright, waiting for you to make a slip and give me away. For God's sake, don't make a slip . . ." He got out. On the left was now the bridge, spanning the neck of the lake, and a single star. The house was humped on the other side, most of its mass in darkness. A street lamp marked the plantain tree. I told Inga:

"We can walk from here."

She sat stiffly and her face looked bloodless in the shadows. I got out and waited for her, paying the driver. Her shoe buckled over on a stone as she left the taxi, and I knew how she felt. There was no strength in her legs.

She seemed about to tell me something but we weren't alone. The taxi had gone and Braun had gone, but certain shadows moved and the night was too calm for even a murmur not to carry. Sounds were on the cold air, audible in the intervals between our footsteps. She walked with me through the gates of the drive, and a man came down from the curve of steps that were lit by the lamp above the doors; his shadow reached us first. Another man came from behind us, and we all climbed the steps in silence.

When I heard the doors close, I knew I had made my throw and would have to stand by it.

Nobody seemed to be clear about what to do with us; three men stood in dark suits, each by a doorway, staring at nothing. There was no baroque here: the hall was immense and furnished as bleakly as a monastery. I said to Inga:

"Show me the shrine."

It would be good for her to let me see it.

Her eyes were large, their pupils dilated in the artificial light. She took a step back from me and then another. "Do you believe," she asked me, "that you'll leave here alive?"

She'd begun shivering again.

"Yes."

She seemed to accept it, and the shivering stopped. Her lips parted to say something more but footsteps were fading in from the marble distances. Two men were advancing on us, marching on us, their feet in unison; they were the kind of men who had never learned to walk.

"You will both accompany us," said one of them.

Fifteen stairs, a mezzanine, ten more stairs. This data was filed mentally with the rest: six average paces from the plantain to the gates, gates twelve feet high and locked back with ball-levers, twenty-seven paces from the gates to the curving steps, reasonable shrub cover, two balconies on the face of the building . . . nineteen paces from the double doors to the staircase . . . so on.

More doors, with our shadows grouped against them.

Permission to enter was begged and received in staccato fashion, correct to the last heel-click, and then I heard the comic and terrible pig-grunt that I had not heard for twenty years: *"Heil Hitler!"* And as the doors opened, I knew that they opened onto the Third Reich.

It wasn't the same room. This was Operations. The map of Europe was thirty feet wide and reached to the ceiling where a battery of spotlights was trained on it. The main plotting table took up a quarter of the room; a dust-cover masked it. The huge curtains were made of blackout fabric and there was the insignia on each of them in white and scarlet: the swastika.

Above the desk where the man sat was a portrait in oils floodlit by concealed lamps in the edge of the jutting frame; not a bad likeness, though the weakness of the mouth had been delicately altered and the eyes had humanity in them. The words were embossed in gold Gothic at the base of the portrait: OUR GLORIOUS FÜHRER.

There were six other men apart from the fat one who sat at the desk. All were in black shirts with a gold swastika on the breast. One was Oktober.

He came toward us. The others didn't move.

Inga pulled the black-covered file from her trench coat pocket and gave it to Oktober. "He's read it," she said. "All of it."

Oktober held the file in both hands. For the first time I saw him hesitate before speaking, and although his blank glass eyes were directed at me there was the impression that he was also looking behind him at the man at the desk. Oktober was in the presence of a superior.

"Make your report," he told Inga. She stood away from me, and looked only at him.

"I received a visit, Reichsführer, from Braun. He had managed to get hold of the file and wanted Quiller to see it and pass it to his

Control." She spoke, I thought, a little like Oktober himself, her harsh Berliner accent whittling at the words. The peripheral glow from the map lamps brightened the gold of her hair and she stood very straight with her heels together. "There was nothing I could do, Reichsführer. My orders were to continue operating in the role of defector whenever in contact with Braun. He—"

"Stop." The word came from the man at the desk like a soft pistol shot. I studied his face. It was simply an eater's face, a devourer's face, the eyes watchful for prey, the mouth long and thin and set between pouches, like a stretched H. "Be more precise."

She had stiffened. "Yes, Reichsleiter. Braun contacted me and asked to meet Quiller. I reported the request to Reichsführer Oktober and was told to allow the meeting. I contacted Quiller and asked him to visit me. Braun came first. A few minutes before Quiller arrived, Braun showed me the file and said he meant to let Quiller have it. There was nothing I could do since it was impossible to contact the Reichsführer by phone in front of him. I was not too worried because I knew there was heavy cover and Quiller couldn't hope to reach his Control with the file—"

"Wait." She stopped immediately. "It must have occurred to you that there was a risk involved. You knew that there was heavy cover. You knew that you had only to use the telephone to ask for situation orders. Well?"

"Both Braun and Quiller would have realized at once that my role of defector was false and that I was in opposition to them. My standing orders to get their confidence and particularly to seduce Quiller morally and physically were of great importance to me, Reichsleiter. I was forced to make my own decision." She paused.

"Proceed."

"Thank you, Reichsleiter. I decided that when Quiller left the apartment I would report the situation at once by phone. With heavy cover in the vicinity, I could have passed on any orders without delay and he could have been caught and put under immediate restraint, and the file taken from him. This was unnecessary. He told us he intended to come here himself, to confirm the information on file. I was unable to understand his reasons, but I believed he meant it. I therefore came with him, so that if he made any attempt to contact his Control, I could signal cover and prevent him. I beg you to consider, Reichsleiter, that my actions were dictated by the highest concern for the success of my personal mission."

Oktober had watched her intently and now seemed satisfied. He was directly responsible for this agent, and any lapse in her efficiency would reflect on him.

The others present also relaxed. The Reichsleiter sat brooding for some seconds, and then he turned his gaze on me.

"You are said to have read the file."

There were three ways to play it: obstinate, worried, or dumb. The first way would be the most expected, with my record of obstinacy with Oktober.

"Yes, I've read it."

"Why did you decide to come here?"

"To get confirmation. The info might have been false. I'd never heard of Braun and I wanted to get him confirmed as well."

"And now you have done that."

"I have."

"What gave you the impression that you could leave here as freely as you came?"

"Experience. I've been trained to get out of places."

He sat with his hands bunched loosely on the desk; they were a child's hands, pink-fleshed, pudgy, designed to clutch at whatever they touched, to possess the world piecemeal so that it need no longer be feared. A ring clung to one finger like a dead blue eye. He said without expression:

"A short time before you arrived, there was a signal from our agents in North Africa. The nuclear test will be set in operation at 2300 hours. That is twenty minutes from now. It is a night operation designed partly to test the effects of radioactivity and its fringe properties in the total absence of sunlight." He got to his feet and moved heavily across to the plotting table. "*Sprungbrett* is similarly a night operation. That is why we are able to avail ourselves of this supreme opportunity. For seven hours the entire Mediterranean area will be in darkness and—according to news reports—under a shroud of radioactive fallout. We shall thus be in sole command of that area even before the operation is launched, since news of that nature will of course create mass confusion and panic."

He took a corner of the dust-cover and jerked it from the plotting table. "You may study the situation for yourself."

I moved to the table. Mediterranean area longitudes 7° W to 35° E, latitudes 32°—42° in relief. All units in red counters assembled eastern seaboard Spain, seaboard Egypt, and the toe of Italy. Blue areas Gibraltar, Algeria, Libya, Israel, Greece, Cyprus, and Sicily. The indications were magnetic-tab.

I gave it a couple of minutes. When I looked up he was gazing at me with his pale-blue glittering eyes.

"What do you think, Herr Quiller?"

I checked the wall clock. "He left it too late. Braun."

"That is so. He had no indication of our timing, and of course it doesn't appear on the file. At this moment our forces are standing by in the operational areas. Within sixteen minutes from now the nuclear test will take place. Within ninety minutes of the news that it has misfired, ten times that many units will have reached the area by troop-transport. German officers commanding are awaiting the signal at this moment." He turned away from the table. "So there is nothing you can do. Nothing. Seven years' meticulous planning has brought us to the brink of this operation, and it cannot be arrested in a quarter of an hour. You have the intelligence to see that."

It had become very quiet in the room.

I said: "I'm not convinced."

He turned to face me squarely and the pale eyes became sparks of light in the pouchy flesh. "It is not my concern to convince you, Herr Quiller. You are a mote in the sandstorm that is about to blow. But I am proud of *Sprungbrett*. It was my conception and I have nurtured it to maturity. It will thus please me to convince you of its invincibility. In a few minutes we shall receive the news that will touch off our operation. From that same instant you will be free to leave. Then you will be convinced that there is *nothing* you can do. You are powerless. You are useless to me and to your Control. You are not, Herr Quiller, worth the expenditure of a single bullet."

He went back to his desk.

It was Inga who spoke, and not to me. She was standing in front of the desk. Her voice was rough. *"Mein Reichsleiter* . . . Let me convince an unbeliever. Let me show him *die Reliquie!"*

The man said nothing. He seemed uninterested in her sudden outburst, but he gazed at her for a moment and then moved a pudgy hand, granting the request.

She waited for me, and I followed her to the far end of the room where I had noticed some curtains. They were a fall of black velvet with the swastika emblazoned on it. She stood erect in her military trench coat, the pride shining from her face.

"You asked me to show you the shrine."

Someone must have operated a switch; the velvet was split and its two halves drew apart. The niche was lighted by a single flame in a bowl of red marble. The relics were cradled in a vessel of clear crystal, and were pure white.

There are various reports on this subject. Witnesses were hard to locate in the holocaust of Berlin at the time. The most authoritative evidence was presented by British Military Intelligence in 1945. It was established that the corpses of Hitler and Eva Braun were burnt in the garden of the Chancellery on the evening of April 30th, but no trace was found of the charred remains. These were removed in secret. A statement by Frau Junge (who was in the Führerbunker during the last hours) said that the cremated relics were collected in a box and secretly taken to the Hitler Youth leader Axmann. The sacred relics would thus be passed on to the next generation, represented by the Hitler Youth.

The light from the small flame was reflected in the crystal, so that the bleached remains were seen as if enwrapped in fire.

Her face was there, too, distorted by the curves of the glass and the flame's movement. She was staring into it. I remembered something she had said when she had first spoken to me of her childhood and the later years when she had defected from Phönix. They had tried to make her go back. "I refused to go back, but I swore on something they keep there that I would never talk." I had known it must be some kind of shrine, something sacred. She had said also: "The only god I had ever been told about was the Führer."

Here was the holy sepulcher.

I watched her face in the crystal. She couldn't move; she could only stare. I knew how many times she must have come here before, to stand silently in communion with those who had peopled her child's world: the "grown-ups" of the doomed Führerbunker— Uncle Hermann, Uncle Guenther, her own mother . . . and her god. She had known them and loved them, and they had turned, before her child's eyes, into creatures stranger than the fiends of a fable; and she herself had become as suddenly a changeling, first a child, then a freak, a werewolf with a child's face.

This much remained of all that she had known as home: cold bones and bitter ash, cradled forever in the chill of glass.

Then her face was suddenly gone and all I could see was her reflected hand, raised and held palm-flattened. From behind me her voice came, a soft screech: *"Heil Hitler!"*

There were other voices, breaking to a murmur of approval, and I turned to see the group of men who stood watching her, moved by her cry of faith.

The black velvet came together silently.

Unnervingly, a telephone began ringing. It was the Reichsleiter who answered. He listened for a few seconds and then nodded, saying only: "Good. Very good." He lowered the receiver tenderly.

To the others he said: "Gentlemen, we must wish ourselves good fortune in our endeavors."

They closed around the desk and one of them took his hand. Oktober spoke to him and was answered. He turned toward me and I watched the steel trap of his mouth open and shut on a shouted order to the man who had never left his post at the doors. "The prisoner will leave. He will not be molested. The order will be passed on."

I looked at Inga before I crossed to the doors. She said nothing. She turned and joined the throng of men at the Reichsleiter's desk.

The guard stood aside for me to pass, and spoke to others outside. The order was passed on as I went down the ten stairs and crossed the mezzanine, went down the fifteen stairs and reached the hall, took the nineteen paces to the entrance doors, and walked through them unchallenged.

The night struck deathly cold against my face. The lamps cast my shadow along the street as I went my way alone. I was free.

I was as free as Kenneth Lindsay Jones had been on the night he had walked out of that house.

20 | THE BUNKERKIND

I walked toward the bridge.

KLJ had been found in the water but they said he'd been shot dead before immersion. Somewhere here, among these shadows where I walked, was the precise spot where he had crumpled to the bullet.

I still believed in my certainties that had led me to make this final single throw, but if some of them were wrong, if only one of them, the smallest, were wrong, my place would be here, too: not at home nor down the road at the crossing nor far across the face of the earth—but here, and now.

It is a feeling that we sometimes have, when we've taken a calculated risk. We think: this move could kill me, so if I assume that it will, if I assume I'm already dead and finished, I won't have to worry or be afraid.

Fear of death can increase the risk of meeting with it, because of stomach-thinking.

Just as I reached the beginning of the bridge, a car came from a side street and got up speed, and as it passed me my nape shrank. The mental (brain-think) decision to assume death and so remove fear is a useful exercise, but the stomach thinks for itself.

The bridge was quiet, a chain of lamps and a gleam of water below. When I heard the footsteps I kept on walking and didn't turn around. There was probably no danger; if they decided to shoot me down they wouldn't hurry to catch me up like this.

They were nearing. I kept on. Then I knew. It was a woman in soft shoes.

"Quill . . ."

I stopped. She looked up into my face, panting. She said: "I had to make a show in front of them."

"Of course."

She gripped my arm. "It must have sounded terrible to you."

"A fraction embarrassing."

Her eyes flickered beyond me, checking shadows. "Please trust me. It's what I came to ask. Trust me."

"I trust you."

If I survived the mission, there would have to be a full report sent in to the Bureau. Under the heading Inga Lindt there would be facts summarized. Give or take a few details the report would read:

First encounter: at the Neustadthalle, Berlin. It was noticed that Lindt left the courtroom just ahead of me. It was likely that the driver of the crush car (see elsewhere) was waiting for a signal that I was coming into the open street, so that he would have time to start the engine and get into gear. It was not thought at the time that Lindt made that signal, but later experience indicated it.

(Oktober mentioned that a *portrait parlant* had been made of me subsequent to my having been seen in the courts—though not in the Neustadthalle. I was thus recognized going in, and Lindt was sent in with orders to leave just ahead of me and make a signal to the crush car. It will be remembered from the earlier sections of this report that the crush attempt was in fact made by a wild-head group in the Phönix organization, so that Lindt's orders would have come from them, not from Oktober. The top directive wanted me alive, for questioning under duress.)

Immediately following the crush attempt, Lindt claimed that it was meant for her. This was an obvious line for me to follow. There was a conversation in her apartment during which she stated that she was a defector from Phönix. It is believed her description of early life and experiences in the Führerbunker were perfectly true. It was now suspected, however, that she was still under the influence of Phönix and might even be one of their operators. This was confirmed by her mentioning to me that Rothstein was in Berlin. My immediate reaction was that (1) she knew I had once known him, (2) had been ordered to drop his name casually, and (3) expected me to talk about him. I did not do this.

It was decided to visit Rothstein and discover if he knew of Phönix, so that I could warn him that they knew his name. There were assistants in his laboratory and it was impossible to talk safely. He appeared to have a need to tell me something, but made no appointment to see me again.

The circumstances of Rothstein's death and my blame for it (by negligence) will be found under that heading. It is relevant to say here that in going to see him (as a direct result of Lindt's mention of his name), I exposed him to their increased suspicion. Had no visit been made, they might well have thought that there had never been any connection between us, and dismissed their suspicions. The fact of Lindt's mentioning his name led finally to his shooting. Thus I was now convinced she was a Phönix agent.

It was decided that I should let her continue to play her part as a defector (anti-Phönix) and that I should seem to continue to accept this. Certain personal feelings toward her were now intruding, but they did not of course interfere in any way with the pursuance of my mission. It was in fact hoped that further contact with her might afford me information on Phönix.

Concerning the attempt by Oktober to force admissions from me in Lindt's apartment by seeming to submit her to physical torture in my presence, the full details will be found under the relevant heading Interrogation. It should be noted here that I became aware that Lindt underwent—at this precise time—a psychological change. My own theories on this may be untenable to a psychologist but they should be detailed in this report, since the whole of my subsequent course of action stemmed therefrom.

Lindt was obsessed with the concept of total strength. As a child she had been given faith in Adolf Hitler and it was no less feverish than was found in millions of her own countrypeople. Following the Führer's suicide, and her own psychical trauma caused by the final hours in the besieged Führerbunker, she retained that faith and was ripe for subsequent indoctrination into the Phönix creed, which derived its very name from the idea that the Führer had risen from his ashes. He was therefore—to Lindt—still a god, and still totally strong. She allied herself with men whom she believed to be unbreakable. (The personality of Oktober—a Reichsführer in the organization—gave an impression of total, unbreakable strength.) It was during Oktober's attempt to interrogate me under pressures induced by my fears for her while she was apparently being tortured in my presence that she met with a psychological confrontation that unbalanced her values. During this interrogation I was aware that (1) she was not in fact suffering distress but lending herself to a new method of inducing me to talk, (2) I must appear to believe that she was being tortured, and (3) I must get out of the corner without revealing that I knew her to be an agent, in case I could use her later as a source of information. (Reference Point 2: the moment I realized that Oktober had come to simulate a torture scene, I *made myself* believe in it, so that all my subsequent actions should appear consistent. This deliberate self-deception was an aid in throwing the faint.)

Having induced genuine syncope by artificial stimuli, I recovered to find Oktober gone, and Lindt sobbing.

It is my theory that when she heard me tell Oktober to go ahead and kill her slowly, but that he would fail to make me talk, she imagined she had found someone as unbreakable as he. (She would have heard of his failure with the narcoanalysis, an additional sign of my reluctance to yield.) The important point here is that although she had always allied herself with men whom she thought were totally strong (unbreakable), she had never seen this characteristic evidenced *in the enemy*. This experience came at a time when our personal relationship had very recently developed to a degree where other psychological influences carried their weight. Thus she suddenly found herse'f allied *to me* and—since I was hitherto an enemy—opposed to Phönix. I believed her fit of sobbing to be rooted in bewilderment (because of severe change in psychic attitudes) and fear (of the retribution to which she herself was now exposed and which an organization as ruthless as Phönix would be quick to mete out).

Untenable though this theory might be in the case of a stable personality, it was the most applicable among many others in the case of a woman long unbalanced by grave trauma in childhood (in the Führerbunker).

For reasons of caution, I kept my beliefs to myself and proceeded as she would have expected, telephoning her doctor and asking him to come at once. (He would be a member of Phönix and she would simply explain to him that his services were not in fact required, as nothing more than simulated torture had been undergone.) Note: the presence of blood on her legs (as evidence to me that the torture had been genuine) had been produced by the slight cutting of the flesh behind one ear lobe. At our next meeting I looked for the scar left by the incision and remarked it; healing was not by that time complete.

Before leaving the apartment, I put my theory about her violent change of loyalties to the test by writing a number on one of her Kleenex tissues and telling her that she could reach me there by phone if she wished. This number—that of a bar named the Brunnen—had been picked at random from the directory while I waited for the doctor to answer. The same night I checked the Brunnen Bar for observers or start-point tags and found none. It was to be expected that one or more would have been posted there if Lindt had given the number to her people. I felt it safe to assume that she had not given it, and her omission confirmed my theory: she was now allied with me.

It was concluded, at about the same time, that Oktober had decided to change his tactics after my exhibition of syncope. The narcoanalyst (Fabian: see under Interrogation) had described to Oktober a technique used at Dachau, whereby information was successfully extracted from people believing themselves to be threatened with certain death. They would be "reprieved" and offered the promise of sexual congress at the height of stimulation (return of life and positive forces granted by "reprieve"). These particular circumstances were in fact my own, not long before: I had been expected to go to Lindt soon after believing that I had been "reprieved" (Grunewald Bridge episode, *q.v.*). Oktober, in my view, had been so impressed with Fabian's technique that when I passed out in the Lindt apartment he went in to her and told her to interrogate me herself on an implied promise of sexual congress. The prospect was the more hopeful since I was thought to be in a state of compassion for her, following the simulated torture session. (It was to increase my compassion that blood drops were then taken from the ear lobe and applied to the inside thighs, indicating to me that an attack had been made on the urethra, in line with classical method.)

She was too distressed mentally by her bewilderment and fear (see foregoing) to tell me that she had now, in truth, defected from Phönix. It would not have been easy for her to explain her position, since she believed that at that time I assumed her to have defected a long time ago. She would simply have told Oktober that she would try out the new tactics, and let him leave the apartment. Her actual breakdown came at that precise moment, leading to the fit of sobbing once we were alone.

From the time when I left her apartment that night, there was a noticeable reduction in tagging and observation. Example: my meeting with Pol was unobserved, and there had been no tag on my journey to the park. It was assumed the adverse party was giving me rope so that I should—being off-guard—try to visit Lindt again. She would then be expected to try their new tactics as ordered by Oktober. I did not go to see her. Their patience became exhausted and she was next ordered to contact me and ask me to see her at the apartment. I then went there and found the agent Helmut Braun. (Note: she had put on clothes of a vivid red. I had seen her only in black, before. I believed this to be an expression—not so much to me as to herself—of her radically altered attitudes (red = life, black = death), and I accepted this as further confirmation of my theory that she was now allied with me and opposed to Phönix. There follows the section on Helmut Braun.

I could hear the water lapping at the legs of the bridge. Helmut Braun? It was difficult to think about him when I stood so close to her.

"There's no time, Quill, to talk. As long as you trust me."

I said: "I do."

She took my hand. Her eyes shone in the lamplight. She said: "Then I can come with you."

"Are you walking out on them?"

"Running. I don't know when you found out I was working for them, but you know when I stopped."

"It hasn't been long."

"But it will be. They suspect me now—that's why I had to give that exhibition in there. I'll be safe if I go with you. Take me."

"I'm going to my Control. There might be time to stop *Sprungbrett* if there's a last-minute hitch. And I've seen their faces, and I know their names. So I've got to send a signal."

"Take me with you. Wherever you go I'll be safe. You're my life, Quill."

I said: "It's no go. There's still a risk. They told me it's too late but they know I'll try to put a signal in to Control, in case there's a last hope. And there's a risk they'll try to stop me."

Her face had gone bleak. "You won't take me?"

"I can't. Not safe."

"It's that you don't trust me." She took her hand from mine.

I looked past her along the span of girders and then looked

again at her face. "Listen to me. This is how much I trust you. There's a risk of their shooting me down if I try to send that signal. If they do, it won't ever reach my Control. Unless you'll help me."

Her head came up. To reassure her I gave a smile. She said nothing.

I told her: "Fix this number in your memory. 02.89.62. Berlin exchange." I made her repeat it twice. "Oktober won't get onto your track for a time—you made a convincing show in there. You're more free than I am, and safer. Phone that number. Give them the code word: *Foxtail*. Tell them about *Sprungbrett*. All of it. Then ask them to pick you up. Once you're with my people, you'll be safe."

"Then . . . I'll see you again?"

"If we both get through."

I kissed her mouth for the last time and turned away and walked quickly to the end of the bridge without looking back, but I knew I would always remember her as she was then, my lost little *Bunkerkind*, slim and erect and triumphant in her soldier's coat with the light on her helmet of hair.

It would take her five minutes to reach the house and report to her Reichsleiter, and five minutes for them to phone that number and find it was a fake. It would give me ten minutes' start on them, and a chance to live.

21 | TRAPSHOOT

In trapshooting, the pigeon is released from the trap and then shot down.

This was my situation now.

I had stopped for a few minutes at the end of the bridge to survey the terrain, and now I had reached a street in Zehlendorf, and stopped again.

One of them was seventy-five yards distant, standing in shadow. Another was closer, waiting some fifty yards in the opposite direction. (It was the pincer trick, one tag rounding a block and keeping ahead. It is useful but can be done only when there are plenty of tags.) A third man was not far from the first. I couldn't see him but I knew where he was because I'd seen him fade. The taxi had pulled up quietly at the intersection and no one got out.

A clock struck eleven. I listened patiently to the strokes, calmed by their measured certainties. It was a half hour since I had left the bridge and so far I'd seen five of them.

There was no hurry. Sometime before dawn, I must get a signal through and do it without their knowledge. On the way from the bridge I had passed four phone-kiosks but couldn't use them. If I went into a kiosk to call up Control in Rabinda-Tanath, I would come out into a hail of fire. They would then go into the kiosk and call up their highest contact in one of the police departments, probably (and preferably) the Kriminalpolizei because they could get a quicker reaction from the Berlin Exchange. The Exchange would be told to find out what number had just been called from the kiosk and to find out the name and address of the subscriber. Phönix would then send a party into Local Control Berlin to seize all papers and personnel.

Phönix was ready to launch a big-scale operation and they couldn't do it before they were certain of how much my Control knew about it. It must be an operation whose success would depend on absolute secrecy and/or surprise. Pol had told me: "If you help us to bring down Phönix, you'll save a million lives and it will almost certainly cost you yours." He had said: "We *do* want information, badly. We want to know where Phönix has its base. *They* want information, too, and as badly. They want to know how much *we* know of their intentions. Their most direct way of getting that information is through you." He had said: "Your mission is to get near enough to see them and signal their position to us, giving us the advantage."

I had believed him at last and still did. They would be waiting now in the room on the ninth floor of the corner building at Unter den Eichen and Rhönerallee with a full staff, waiting for me to signal. The line would be open to London. Phönix was also waiting for me to signal, so that they could locate Local Berlin and wipe it out before my people could reach their base and wipe out Phönix. It was my own situation in macrocosm: the kill and the overkill.

There were no more doubts that Phönix did in fact intend launching a big-scale operation: they were taking immense trouble with me, keeping me alive and hoping to crack me open by one method after another. I was the third operator to have been assigned to this one mission. They had let Charington get too close and had killed him off early. They had given Kenneth Lindsay Jones more rope—he'd been within rifle-shot of their base when they had killed him. Now they had let me right in and let me go again, matching my last single throw.

I was now certain that KLJ had died because he'd been working with a contact. He had approached that contact within sight of the

Phönix base and Phönix had panicked and shot them both. (It is not easy, even in Berlin, to dispose of a corpse. Probably they had managed to get a sinker around the contact, but KLJ was found floating.) He had got so close to base (and had possibly been let in and out again, as I had been) that the risk of his passing his information to Control was too high, and it was a double risk because of the contact.

Now they were going the limit because their need to locate Local Berlin was fully urgent. *Ergo*, the time for the launching of their operation must be getting very short.

It would have been Oktober who had triggered the present situation. He had lost patience when Inga had failed to report any success in interrogating me on the Dachau principle, which she had been ordered to do. He had decided to try me with the file on *Sprungbrett*. Helmut Braun had been sent in with it to convince me that he was a defector, as I was thought to believe Inga herself.

The file trap had possibly been tried on KLJ, in which case I was surviving him only because I had no contact. It may have been simply that they didn't have sufficient tags to cover him and his contact safely. Tonight they had five working on me, probably more.

Sprungbrett didn't look too bad on paper, and they wouldn't expect a field operator to have much knowledge of military strategy. But there were some obvious flaws and it was then that I decided on my single throw, gambling on the assumption that the file had been given freely into my hands in order to force me into action. I was to grab it and try to get it to my Control and make the touchdown before they tripped me.

Their risk was slight: *Sprungbrett* was a faked file, got up specially for me, and if I managed to reach Control with it I'd have wasted my time. But it would give them a chance to locate my base by tagging me to whatever point of contact I made.

I'd never seen Braun or a photograph of Braun. I had been sure that Inga was still allied with me but too scared to make a move in front of Braun. I think she would have told me that the *Sprungbrett* file was a fake if it had been possible to talk. It wasn't. First Braun, then the man in the lift, then Braun again in the taxi. He must have been worried when I said I was going into the Phönix base. He had no orders to cover that one. So he stayed behind us in the apartment and either made a quick phone call or tipped off one of the tags that were by that time thick in the area. The message had gone into the Phönix base: *Quiller is on his way.*

They were thrown off balance. They had covered the area with heavy tagging, given me the file, and sent me along the path to my base. Now I was heading for theirs.

Braun left the taxi first and went straight in to see Oktober without my knowledge (he was a "defector"). He told him I had arrived outside. Decision: to carry on with the same game. I'd read the file and wanted confirmation. I would have it.

Inga and I were kept waiting in the hall. In the operations room they set up the map table for the Mediterranean Area and positioned the markers: a ten-minute undertaking with a section-leaf table of that kind where a dozen maps can be slipped in and out together with the magnetic strips.

They brought me in.

A defector is a creature as peculiar as the chameleon. He will tend to take on the color of his environment. In the London Bureau we had a man who worked with us for five years and defected during a mission in Tangier. Two weeks and he was back with us and we knew what had happened but didn't tell him. He was sent out again under cover that he didn't suspect, and three days later we sat listening to the tape: he had met the adverse party again and talked to him in a room where we had miked the ceiling fan. He told the adverse party that he had defected: *yet we knew by his actions that he was now back on his mission and doing a fine job for us.* But we'd shut down on him and he found out and hanged himself on the iron grille of a shrine in the Iglesia San Augustino.

Normally, a true defector will get out and stay out unless great pressures (financial or political) add their influence to his already uncertain values. Then he will either double or bounce and they mostly bounce. Our man hanged himself because he'd lost direction and couldn't find his way home because he no longer knew what home was.

The most common instances are less spectacular: a man will defect, take one look at the terrain on the other side, and make for home again, chastened and sobered. He is like a man who swears one day he'll have himself a whore and gets to the top of the stairs and then makes a bolt for it.

The prevalent factors bearing on defection are moral, political, sometimes financial, religious, and sexual (particularly homosexual). Inga was influenced by none of these pressures. She was character-motivated. She was not a true defector. She thought she was. She even put on red slacks to prove it. Then she lost direction and had to head for home—because she still knew where home was. A crystal of ashes.

And when I had told her I was going into the Phönix base she'd begun shivering, because when the crash came she was going to be there to watch it. She was going to be a part of it herself. She was going to reestablish herself with all the protestative violence of the true repentant, and shift the guilt onto a sacrificial victim. So she took the file and handed it over and said: "He's read it. All of it."

Not that it mattered. She hadn't known I was meant to read it. Braun would have been under orders not to tell her. She was already coming close to being suspected of defection and probably knew it. Oktober was wondering why she had made no attempt to contact me and interrogate me on the Dachau principle as instructed, and why she had drawn no scrap of information from me since the time of the crush attempt, when she was given the mission.

Certainly she hadn't been trusted to escort me alone to the Grunewald base: Braun had come with us and hadn't left us until we were within earshot of new cover. She knew this and her fears increased, and her fit of fervor in the presence of the sacred ash was a desperate attempt to convince them of her unwavering faith.

Here in the chill streets the night was sane again, with none of the mad overtones of that house with its swastika trappings and its vestiges of the Führerbunker. Yet this whole city was mad, however much it was denied by mere acceptance. Not far from here the Russian war memorial stood inside the British boundary, so that it was agreed that barbed wire should surround it. A Russian sentry guarded the memorial and a British sentry guarded the barbed wire. To the north, in Spandau Prison, thirty men of four nations—British, French, American, and Russian—guarded Hess, Speer, and von Schirach: a hundred and twenty armed soldiers guarding three old men the world had long forgotten. Beside such monuments of absurdity, the renaissance of a Nazi group with illusions of making war seemed almost rational.

Thoughts of Inga came again because after half an hour I could still feel the touch of her mouth. There was a question left in my mind and I had to clear it even though it couldn't alter my position or immediate actions. Of three possible answers, one seemed most apt: she had followed me from the house to the bridge for her own purposes, not under orders. She knew that her organization had suspected her of defecting. She hoped that by coming with me to their base, by handing them the file, and by hailing the burned bones of their common god she had convinced them of her faith: but she couldn't be sure.

They needed urgently to locate my Control. If she could locate it herself and report her success to them, she would no longer go in fear of them; they would accept her and honor her. Therefore she had made a final effort to persuade me that she was still a defector whose faith now rested solely in me. ("You're my life, Quill," she had said.) Perhaps she believed that because of what had happened between us on that innocent afternoon, I could still be undermined. It might have been so. She had begged me to take her with me . . . and she knew where I was going: to my Control.

I had played it her way because it might conceivably be useful to me. If Phönix went on thinking they'd convinced me that Operation *Sprungbrett* was genuine, they would continue their present tactics. Dangerous though these tactics were to myself, they were known to me and I could take whatever opposing action I thought fit. If they changed these tactics, I would no longer be in control of the situation.

Inga would have reported that I was indeed convinced about *Sprungbrett*. The number I had given her had nothing to do with Local Berlin. It was an impromptu jumble of figures. If such a number existed they would get a reply, but still find it belonged to some unknown subscriber. But they wouldn't be sure: they would check with the Exchange and send a couple of men to the address to make certain it wasn't Local Berlin playing hard to get. They would finally consider the possibility that Inga had made a mistake with the number I gave her, since it was verbal.

The chances, then, of their pursuing their present tactics were if anything increased.

Small comfort: these men meant my death.

I had been safer in that house than here in the open city. I had known that since they were forcing me to signal Control they must let me leave there alive, and try sending that signal more urgently than ever, now that I knew where their base was and that it possessed a full-scale operations room.

Going into that house I had not looked for death. I looked for it now.

There was a sixth man, a new one in a light-colored coat. I watched him and he watched me. He would be one of the decoys. Out of a total of maybe twenty tags, only one or two would be briefed to make the kill. This was straight Oktober-thinking and I felt comfortable about it. I had been released from the pigeon trap and they had to tag me; they knew I would spot their tags because the hour was late and the streets emptying; therefore they went the whole hog and plastered the place. Soon they would begin calling them off, one by one, letting me flush half a dozen to keep me happy . . . until, sometime between now and dawn, I would believe I was alone and would make a bid to signal Control. Then they'd be there, the last of them, and I wouldn't see them coming.

If I made my signal and they saw me do it, they would shoot me within the next sixty seconds. If I delayed too long they would start worrying, as they did with Charngton and KLJ, and would shoot me and switch off the risk. I didn't think they'd tag me beyond dawn, so I assumed that to be my deadline.

Meanwhile, Local Berlin and London would be waiting for me to signal. So would Phönix.

I knew now why they had sent Pol to bring me the KLJ report. They had to convince me, on field-executive level, of my position. And Pol had described for me the precise situation that existed now. He had said: "We are worried that you don't understand your position. It is this. There are two opposing armies drawn up on the field, and you are in the gap between them. That is where you are, Quiller. In the gap."

22 | CORNER

By four o'clock in the morning I knew I was beaten. There was a strange relief in the knowledge.

We had done the whole city. In five hours we must have gone thirty or forty kilometers on foot and in a dozen taxis from north to south, Hermsdorf to Lichtenrade, from east to west, Neukölln to Spandau, and through seventeen hotels and three stations, to finish where we'd started in Zehlendorf.

The eyes gave in first: I saw dark specks on light surfaces. The eyes and the nerves. I had flushed ten of them before three o'clock and one of these ten had tried so hard to stick that I knew he couldn't be a decoy. In two of the hotels, I had gone as far as asking the night porter to deliver a message for me but the message was never written because I sensed they were on to me.

My coat was torn and one knee was swelling: there'd been ice between the lines at the Hauptbahnhof freight yard and I'd slipped between a truck and a loading jig full of unplaned timber. One glove was missing and a button was gone from the coat: I'd tried topping a pair of iron gates at the Kaulsdahl Cemetery but it had been no go. Sometime about midnight we had started a scare at Checkpoint Charlie because I'd given a taxi driver fifty marks to keep his foot down and he'd got blocked at the east end of the Friedrichstrasse and simply did a U-turn under the nose of the guards.

I was never alone in the open street. Whenever I got a taxi there was another one tagging it, sometimes two or three. There was no point in asking a driver to get a message through to Control: every time I left a taxi they moved in on the driver and questioned him with their gun hands lumpy in their pockets. Every car had a radio and the temptation was very great, but it would be fatal to send out a call to the fleet switchboard because every time they took a car to follow mine they'd order their driver to call his base and request monitoring. No go.

The only time I had come near to flushing the whole team was when I had got a fifty-yard start in the open and headed for the nearest cover—the ruins of the Reichstag; then I'd stepped on broken glass and two guards came over from near the Russian memorial and began using their lamps.

Now we were back in Zehlendorf and in two hours it would be dawn. Three of them were still with me and they would be the fullbacks, briefed to kill. My night was drawing short.

Once the daylight came they wouldn't let me run them any further because there was the risk of losing me in the rush-hour traffic, and they knew that the minute I'd flushed them I would send my signal, and the Grunewald base would be raided straight away and with no chance of an overkill. I had two hours left before Oktober sent them the order to put me in the crosshairs and switch off the risk.

Instinct: go home.

It was nine kilometers and I took a taxi as far as the Lankwitzstrasse and walked from there. Two of them kept up the tag while the third questioned my driver. A light burned in the doorway of the Hotel Zentral and I went in by that entrance and not through the courtyard where the lock-up garages were.

The night porter was cleaning a pair of shoes and looked for my key on the board. I said I had it with me and he said I ought to leave it at the desk when I went out and I said I must remember to do that.

I locked the door and looked around. The room had been

searched but nothing was missing. They had even probed the tube of toothpaste for microfilm: the needle had raised a ridge from the inside.

There was a chance in a thousand of posting a report to Eurosound so I spent twenty minutes at it, locating the Grunewald base and giving a résumé of the *Sprungbrett* affair. The main section of the report dealt with my ideas on what I had now come to think of as the Parallel Assumption, reference the Rothstein document. The fake *Sprungbrett* file had confirmed some of these ideas and there was quite a bit of underlining in my report, because the thing looked weird on paper and London would give it a very sidelong glance.

The factors on which Phönix would have to work were (1) opportunity, (2) local situation in main attack area, (3) availability of armed forces in strength, and (4) security. Therefore the Med was out. There was only one area in the world where the armed forces of East and West were looking down each other's gun-barrels on a cold war footing, and where opportunity + local situation + availability of strength could trigger off a small-scale but developing war. Berlin. The fourth factor—security—was the only doubtful runner, partly because I myself was busy trying to break down the Phönix security to a point where they could no longer risk launching an operation of any kind in any place.

If I could post this report it could be decisive. Wipe out Phönix and the Nazi elements of the German General Staff would be left without central direction.

It was clear that if this were not so, Phönix would not be concentrating on me so fiercely.

The chances against successful transmission being a thousand to one, I didn't waste too much time in neat phrasing. The facts would have to do.

Twenty minutes with the feet on the bed. Brain-think session. Dark specks crossed the trellis-pattern wallpaper and I closed my eyes. Findings: must disregard likelihood of my death. Must not put the Bureau at risk by simply sending a signal (thus committing suicide) and counting on my people making the overkill, because they might not have the time. If suicide-type signal sent, it *must* be phoned in direct, because if this report were seen to be put into a box they would smash open the box, note the address, and start a careful investigation of the Eurosound staff until they found our man; then they would grill him till he spoke or broke. Consider possibility of phoning Captain Stettner: tell him to phone Control for me. Result: tags would go through the routine, kill me off, phone their contact in the Polizei, get him to ask the Exchange what number I had called, find it was Stettner's, and send in a party to snatch him and grill him. (Danger here particularly great since their Polizei contact would probably be higher in rank than captain and would simply order the man to repeat my message.) Consider other possibilities. There weren't any.

Time was 4:35. Eighty-five minutes (it was coming down to minutes now instead of hours) before dawn. The rush hour wouldn't start until eight o'clock but they wouldn't wait for that because they knew that I *would* wait. If I hadn't flushed them by first light, I'd have the sense to cool my heels until the rush hour began and then have another go. That would be Oktober-thinking.

My brain had to be geared to Oktober-thinking or the bastard would do for me.

Oktober-think. Brain-think. The knee was throbbing. The spots flew quietly across the trellis-pattern like slow bullets.

We have arranged a cover man for you.

I don't want a cover.

What happens if you get into a corner?

I'll get out again.

Too bloody confident, that was Quiller.

The room was getting smaller, and I got up. The sweat was starting. Eighty minutes.

There was only one thing to do and that was the thing I hadn't succeeded in doing for the past five and a half hours. I had to signal Control without their seeing me do it.

Paramount consideration: protect the Bureau from risk. Worst eventuality: death and no signal sent, my people back where they began. (Who would replace me? Dewhurst? Disregard likelihood.)

Program: send signal by direct phone *if absolutely certain unobserved*. If impossible, wait for the bullet in the neck and try to . . . (disregard).

I left the glove on the bed. Very fast driving and maze-tactics would be hampered by uneven hand-control. The glove chanced to fall palm-upward on the coverlet and it looked like an appeal, though I couldn't think for what. More time perhaps. Seventy-nine minutes.

The layout of the hotel had been studied the day after I'd moved in. Main entrance, double doors to the terrace, single door from the kitchens, single door to the courtyard. I left the room without a sound, taking five or six minutes with the handle. The corridor was carpeted. There might be one or more adverse parties inside the building, might not. They knew where I'd gone and they knew they'd see me come out again. The phone would be wiretapped, but although they'd searched the room they hadn't miked it, so there wouldn't be anyone looking after a speaker or tape.

The hollow rasping of the "shoe-brush" was the only sound on the stairs. He had the lot to do: night porter and "boots" combined.

It was possible to reach the single door to the courtyard without going within sight of the desk, and I moved only when the "brush" sounded, freezing in the intervals of silence. The door was locked but the key was on the inside.

Chill air. The surface of the yard was concrete and I put my shoes on again and left the door unlocked on principle: insure availability of exits and entrances.

A glass roof covered half the yard, running from the wall of the hotel to the row of lock-ups. Observation was possible only from the hotel windows and the four windows of the house opposite the yard gates. Five minutes to allow the eyes fully to accommodate. Five minutes to check each window. There was no lamp burning in the yard and I stood in eighty percent darkness, stars giving the only light.

There was no observation. The thought was chilling. There should be observation. Recheck windows, shadow areas. No observation. Disregard.

The lock-ups were communal and had two big double doors facing the hotel wall at some sixty feet. Both sets of doors had the same key. The 230 SL pagoda-top was inside the doors nearer the gate and street. It would be possible to open them quietly but not silently; I had oiled the lock, hinges, and swing-bar staple the first time I had run the BMW in here. But there was no point in taking pains. If they were going to open fire as I drove through the gates, they'd have plenty of warning because of the noise of starting up. To open the doors quietly would reduce the warning period by a good ten seconds (time taken to go through the open doorway, get into the Mercedes, and start up). But they would still have fifteen left (time taken to engage reverse, back out, stop, engage first, and move off to the gates). And you can raise a rifle on target from across the knees in one second flat.

But my chances were so slight that I took pains with the doors. A chip of stone got jammed underneath the second one and made a soft screech that echoed under the big glass roof. I was relieved in a way. I had shown my hand and there might be reaction from them, establishing known conditions. I walked from the doors to the gates to get some idea of what these conditions were. There was no risk in this that I wasn't already faced with. Either they would let me drive the car out or they wouldn't. If they wouldn't, I'd be sitting in it, here at this spot, my hands on the wheel, dead, two minutes from now. That was the risk and it wasn't increased by standing here exposed. If they meant to let me drive the car out, they wouldn't fire either now or when I was behind the wheel.

Luminous dial at 5:03. Fifty-seven minutes left.

Oktober-thinking was no go. Even he was sometimes faced with a choice of decisions. He—or his Reichsleiter—would now be deciding whether to let me use the car (so that they could tag me and see me signal Control) or to switch off the risk the moment I got into the car (so that they could relax and think out a new way of locating my base—perhaps using my successor).

The night was still calm. Very far away the throb of a Diesel truck sounded; even more distantly there was a shunt going on in the freight yards. In my area there was total silence. I stood between the gates with the horror coming into me slowly, and when I tried to keep it back it made ever faster return. The left eyelid began.

They had been called off.

Nobody, not even the least efficient field scout in the most tumble-down intelligence service, could fail to see me framed in these gates with the light of a street lamp on me. And to see me they must show themselves, by however small a fraction. The terrain was bare and geometrical, a pattern of ground surface, walls, doors, windows, and roofs; and I gave it a one hundred percent examination. There was no window open even an inch. Every door was shut. The lamp stanchion was less than a foot in diameter except at the base, which stood two feet from the pavement: no cover. The outline of the estate car parked on the other side of the street was utterly distinct and unspoiled. The horizon line was unbroken from roof to roof.

In ten minutes I had reobserved. Nil.

Known conditions had ceased.

Eliminate two considerations: (1) They were not waiting for me farther off, at each end of the street, because there was no absolute guarantee of picking off the driver of a car accelerating at full bore and tire-targets were tricky. The 230 SL would be pitching up eighty kph in third gear by the time it reached either end of this street. (2) They wouldn't be set up to fire from behind a closed window (where reflection could mask them in this light), because deflection is always a risk, the structural quality of the glass being variable. Nor would they be absolutely certain of drilling the pagoda-top roof dead on target from any height. If they were going to fire on me from a closed window they'd do it now, because the door of the garage had raised enough sound to travel through the glass of any window in this area and they'd know my intention: to use the car.

They had been called off.

The eyelid was bad now so I stopped thinking and moved back across the yard and went into the garage through the wide open doors. The same factors applied: there was no *increased* risk in walking through these doors if in fact they'd posted a man in here with orders to kill me off if I tried to get into the Mercedes.

No shot. No sound. No sign.

The awful thing was that I wanted badly to get clear and they were going to let me and I didn't like it or trust it.

Perfectly still. Breathe shallow. Examine.

Sound: the last of the Diesel throb, fading north. Metal on metal from the freight yards. All.

Vision: blurred outlines, three cars, oil drum, wall map, tap, and trough. All.

Scent: petrol, oil, rubber, sacking, timber. All.

Nothing out of place.

Only the voice inside me saying, *I don't like this I don't like this.* Shuddup. Brain-think not stomach-think, getting old, old enough to die.

Luminous dial at 5:24. Thirty-six minutes to go.

Brain-think: make all usual checks and then recheck and then get out, win or lose.

I travel light but sometimes life or lesser but important things depend on vision at night, so I carry a pen torch with three long-life cells and an inverse lens for needle focus. The hood slid up without a click on the felt-lined barrel. The thin beam began moving about. Doors not tampered with. Check interior: all switches and levers in position as left. No foreign odors.

Ten minutes on the interior. Then I opened the luggage compartment and checked contents. Cleared. The engine cover made a slight noise because of the sprung catch, and I stood still for three minutes listening.

The ray probed the engine. Check for recently laid wiring, unfamiliar components, foreign odors. Cleared.

I stood for a minute to steady the breathing. Sweat was gathering at the waist. The bruised knee pulsed. Eyelid calm because action was soothing the nerves.

Right—risk the rest and get in and drive like hell and hope for luck.

Never throw blind.

Back to the interior, checking beneath the fascia panel for new wiring at the ignition and head-lamp switch-points. Cleared.

Keep on working, take advantage of the analogy: I had thought of an analogy, excellent piece of brain-think. The ray probed along the cement floor, picking up chips of stone, ancient splinters rotted dark, the tarnished brass terminal of a sparking-plug, Bosche-type.

Then I got down flat on my back and pulled myself under the chassis and found it at once.

23 | SIGNAL ENDS

The needle ray of light made a circle on the plastic casing. The brass posts of the solenoids were flush-cut and the light gave them a gold shine. There was a slinging-eyelet cast integrally. Apart from these three features it was simply an elegant oblong six-by-three, about the size of a small pocket lamp.

It was Japanese. The last time I had seen one was in Paris in '59 when the Deuxième Bureau handed over the FLN problem to the Main Rouge. It was the same type of bomb that they had used to remove Puchert, and it was the same method: he was blown to pieces in his car on the Guiollettstrasse, Frankfurt, at 9:15 A.M., March 3rd.

Now I was looking at one of these things again. Small, compact, beautifully molded, it could rock a street.

I had expected to find it—and had looked for it—because of the analogy, which was: they've cleared out of here as if there were an unexploded bomb in the place.

The chill of the concrete was seeping through my coat into my shoulder blades but I lay there for half a minute to do some thinking. Oktober was a human computer and this idea would appeal to him. He didn't trust humans who were not computers. He had envisaged the remote possibility of my being unobserved when I finally got around to using the Mercedes in a last attempt to break clear. The orders were that if I had made no signal by first light I was to be switched off. Declining to chance even a remote possibility of failure in this, my death was to be arranged with precision: it was to be *automatic*.

The sweat was dangerous now and I wiped my hand on my coat before reaching up and taking the bomb from its perch on top of the exhaust pipe. The setup was that when I started the engine the vibration of the pipe would dislodge the bomb within the first few minutes of driving and it would hit the ground. Even at high speed the thing *must* fall immediately below the car.

I held it snug on my chest and slid out from under, standing up and listening from sheer habit. The night was mine.

The lock-ups were communal, with only three main partitions six feet high, and there was a side door at the far end, so I checked the gear for neutral and started the engine, moving round to the front of the car and resting the bomb on the slope of the bonnet about a third of the distance from the front edge, where the smooth plastic would slide on the smooth cellulose, given time. The engine was cold and the vibration at its highest. I stood and watched the bomb in the light of the torch. In fifteen seconds it began to slide and I kept my hand ready in case. Twenty seconds and it sped up and reached my hand.

I wanted roughly one minute, so I put the bomb a couple of inches higher than the first time and left it there, climbing the first partition and dropping over, climbing the second and dropping, kicking over an oil tin and disregarding the noise, climbing the third partition and making for the side door. It had a Yale-type lock with a knurled knob and there was an interior bolt in addition; I had oiled them both when I had seen to the big double-doors two days ago.

When I was outside I shut the door after me and sat down with my back to the garage wall. There would be no breaching of the wall itself because of the partitions, but most of the roof would get up and go and there'd be a certain amount of old-fashioned brick-dust-and-splinter fallout.

I could hear the engine of the Mercedes throbbing very faintly. Sixty seconds had gone by. I went on waiting, and thought: London isn't going to like this. There was a lot of private property in the place. But Pol had said a million lives, so London would have to lump it.

Ninety seconds. I had misjudged the slope of the bonnet, put the thing too high. The throb of the engine was settling, with the automatic choke easing off and the mixture thinning. The sharpness of carbon monoxide soured the air. Time-check: 5:49. Eleven minutes to zero but that didn't come into it now. Along the high wall that made one boundary of the courtyard there was the first light of the new day showing; a spire pointed its gray finger at a star. Far away the sounds from the freight yards were getting louder. Then the first cock crowed.

Two minutes. Either there was a resinous adhesion setting up between the plastic and cellulose or the thing had slid to one side and was lodged in the trough of the fairing. If it had lodged, it might stick there forever or it might go on creeping and finally drop. I didn't want to go and have a look. The engine was barely audible now; the temperature gauge would have moved out of the cold sector; oil pressure would be dropping a fraction.

There would be three phases. Initial percussion, audible blast, and air shockwave. Fire was a certainty because of all the petrol about.

Two minutes and a half. The sweat glands began working again. There was absolutely no way of timing a check-up safely; the whole thing would have to be worked out by chemistry (plastic-cellulose inter-reaction, allowance for heat change due to warming of engine), kinetics (movement of bomb across slope of bonnet, references weight, momentum potential of mass, gradient of slope), vibration theory (effect of given rate of mechanical oscillation by metal of bonnet against given mass), and algebra (terms of deduction in all three spheres). A whole team of picked scientists could sit here for weeks without succeeding in telling me *when* it would be safe for me to go and find out what was happening to that *bloody* thing.

Three minutes. The light was strengthening on the far spire and the matt uniformity of the sky was curdling into cloud.

If nothing happened in another ten minutes, I'd have to go and take a look because they'd start moving in on the same principle and I couldn't afford to—

Three phases now operating. Percussion—the ground shook and the wall shuddered at my back. Audible blast—a crash of wild music as the roof went up and the glass over the courtyard shattered and fell away in a drift to the ground. Air shockwave—the hot wind of it fanned past my face, stinking of sodium-chlorate.

I stayed where I was until the yard was ringed with people standing agape in the light of the flames, then I edged my way behind them. Another fuel tank went up and the first fire-bells began sounding from the distance. Then the clock in the spire chimed six.

The taxi put me down in the Unter den Eichen and I went into the passage next to the hat shop, using the double-edged key. We had a notice on the service-lift saying it was out of order, to discourage people. The ninth-floor button operated the lift and also switched on a red winking lamp in both rooms.

Five people were there including Hengel. They looked pasty and red-eyed because they'd been up all night waiting for me to signal. There was a tray of cups so I said: "Have you got some coffee?"

Hengel was already using the direct-line telephone, asking for Pol.

They kept looking me up and down and I remembered I was still wearing the white chef's coat. There would have been a whole bunch of tags in the crowd watching the fire and I'd had to get clear unrecognized.

I took off the coat and dropped it over a chair. We all talked a bit, and in ten minutes Pol came, while I was holding my second cup of coffee in both hands to warm them. A chef's coat isn't much for a winter morning.

Pol had just gone to bed after the night shift and Hengel had got him out again. The room had gone very quiet. A hot operator doesn't just show up at Control just to ask for coffee.

I gave Pol the report I'd written during the early hours at the hotel and they all watched him reading it. He said:

"This will do for a start."

"It's all you'll get for the moment."

He told someone to get onto London, and while we waited he said: "We'll have to go in, you know." He was speaking in English and I thought again of England and how much I needed her.

I said: "Give me till noon. Then you can go in."

"Why noon?" His featureless face was blanker than ever without the glasses.

"I need the time."

He dropped the report onto a desk and asked for copies.

"It depends on London," he told me.

I was feeling tired so I said: "Just for a few hours, London depends on me."

The call came through and they gave me the phone. I talked for a minute and finally had to persuade him. "You can send them in if you have to, sir, but we shall go off at half-cock unless you can give me till noon. Once you raid their base they'll try to put calls out and they might succeed. Give me till noon and I'll give you the whole setup."

He said I was putting a gun at their heads. Bloody fool. We had guns at all our heads. He asked if I couldn't make it earlier than noon.

"I'll try, sir. It should work out well before that, but it's just a reasonable deadline for me to aim at."

He still went on nagging and I had one of my regrettable impulses: "Things got very tricky, sir. I even had to blow up a garage and seven cars, all private property." I listened for a minute to give myself the pleasure and then handed the phone to Pol.

While Pol was trying to smooth things over, I drank some more coffee and asked someone to get me the Public Prosecutor on the other phone.

"Which one?"

"Ebert."

I could hear the phone ringing for a long time and then the Generalstaatsanwalt came on. His voice was perfectly alert, though it was still only a quarter to seven. I asked if I could see him.

"It must be very urgent, Herr Quiller."

"Yes."

He said he was at my disposal and I rang off.

Pol had finished with London.

"They don't like it," he said.

"Do them good."

"I don't like it either."

So they were all going to nag. I drank the coffee as fast as I could without burning my tongue. I would need the caffeine because I would be feeling the fatigue as the work of the morning went on. I was going to do something for the first time in my life and it would be very unpleasant.

"You'll be all right," I told Pol.

"We shall be here until noon, of course." He almost said "at our posts." I knew he would keep the rest of them there, too, to help him sweat it out. All the time I was on the loose there was the danger of being picked up and made to talk. They had lived with this over their heads ever since Pol had given me the Q memorandum, but now it was worse for them because time was running short. They didn't want to be sitting here like so many ducks when Phönix sent a party up here in the lift, or opened fire from the windows across the street with a battery of submachine guns. They didn't want to be picked off one by one as they left the passage by the hat shop, dropping cold onto the pavement before they could warn the next man out.

It wasn't easy for them and they had my sympathy. I always get on better with a Local Control, wherever it is, than those bloody people in London.

I told Pol: "You won't see any adverse action. There's no risk. They think I'm dead. They're still watching the flames. They won't look for me again. So don't worry."

The London line began ringing. He answered the call and did a lot of listening, then hung up. He told me:

"They've signaled British Military H.Q. Berlin. At twelve noon today the Commandant is sending four armored cars to the Grunewald base with fifty troops."

"London always did get the fidgets when there's a flap on." I looked down from one of the windows. The street was filling with traffic. "Will you please phone me a taxi? And has anyone got an overcoat my size?" It looked cold down there, and my own coat was hanging on a peg in the kitchens of the Hotel Zentral.

Sleet was falling again as I crossed the pavement and got into the taxi, right in the middle of the Zeiss close-focus square-15's they had up there. But there would be no tags. I was dead.

Ebert opened the door himself as a gesture of courtesy and invited me to take breakfast with him.

"You have an important client for me, Herr Quiller?"

He was more jovial at the breakfast table than in his office. I said: "Several, Herr Generalstaatsanwalt. We shall be notifying you later in the day." He gave me a long look from under his pink and blond eyebrows, then took another slice of pumpernickel. I remembered he didn't really know who I was. "But I came to ask you a favor," I said. "There is a man I would like to talk to, and you could probably arrange the introduction. He is Bundesminister Lobst."

Ebert ruminated, saw no connection, gave it up, and said:

"Certainly I shall arrange it."

"At his office, as early as possible. I imagine he gets there about nine, being a busy man."

"We will see."

The territories of Ebert and Lobst abutted, and they would know each other well in their official capacities. This was why I had come to Ebert, whom I trusted and who trusted me.

He made two telephone calls and said that I would be shown into the Bundesminister's office on arrival at any time after nine o'clock. The Generalstaatsanwalt would be glad if I would convey to the Bundesminister his personal greetings.

There were forty-five minutes to go, so I found an early barber and had a shave, manicure, and neck-trim to take the fatigue away. It was nine o'clock precisely when I was shown into the Bundesminister's office. He was speaking on a telephone, and his secretary had quietly gone away before he finished the call and turned in his chair and looked at me, but I had been prepared for the secretary still to be here so it would have been all right anyway.

He just sat there without moving or reaching for a drawer, so I took my time crossing to his desk. He started to get up, and I moved around the desk and brought my right hand flattened and palm down and very fast against the side of the neck, taking off some of the force at the last inch so that he wouldn't be under for too long.

Then I left him and locked both doors and came back and sat on his desk.

"Zossen," I said, "I want to know everything."

It made me angry: he just sat there with his eyes turned up a little, trying to focus on my face; but he was a man like that, who never lowered himself to physical action. He gave the orders and signed the papers and left it to his henchmen to do the work.

His eyes were getting their focus now and he said loosely: "It was reported that you were dead." I studied his face. It was worse than cruel: it was greedy. It was an eater's face, a devourer's, the eyes watchful for prey, the mouth long and thin and set between pouches, like a stretched H. It wasn't his face I had recognized in the Grunewald operations room, but his walk, when he had moved from the desk to the map table. Then I had looked at the face again and seen the ice-blue of Zossen's eyes set in the blubber of twenty years of greed.

This face had a third identity and it was public: I had seen it on the front pages of newspapers when Bundesminister Ernst Lobst had made a speech or greeted a visiting diplomat on the Tempelhof field. Thus I had known where to find him. I had come here in case he got wind of the raid at noon today and went to ground. I had come here to make him tell me everything, in case the raid misfired. And I had come here in the name of three hundred nameless men to whom he had once said: "I am due back in Brücknerwald in one hour, for luncheon."

He was fully conscious again and watching me. I told him to speak to his secretary on the interoffice line and give orders that he must on no account be disturbed for the next hour. As he pressed down the switch, I said softly:

"The doors are locked. If you say the wrong thing I shall have a full minute before they break the doors down. I can do a lot to a man like you in sixty seconds. Be careful."

He spoke to his secretary and I was angry with him again because he was so helpless. I must remember the men of Brücknerwald. I must do what I came to do, even though he was helpless.

He closed the switch and I said: "Now you will tell me everything. Everything."

It was not quite ten o'clock when I left the office of the Bundesminister: the work had been quicker than expected. I had not taken a gun with me, nor any weapon at all; but we are not gentlemen, and we have our little ways. He had held out for close on twenty minutes and then broken, asking for mercy. Then he had told me everything.

On the way to the Unter den Eichen, I phoned Captain Stettner at the Z Bureau. "I have someone for you." He didn't sound surprised when I told him the name. There was more than one Bundesminister on the Z Commission files. "I should go and pick him up straight away."

I knew he wouldn't be able to make a decent snatch because it was a job for the *Selbstmord* department, as it had been with Schrader, though in this case there hadn't been a gun. I just wanted it on record that I had last seen the Bundesminister alive.

Pol was still there when I went up to our place. He looked worried at seeing me so early: it was not yet half past ten, and I had stipulated noon.

"What has gone wrong?"

"Nothing," I said. "Set up the tape."

They were all watching me obliquely and I kept my eyes down. I was bloody well fed up with them. When the tape was running I said:

"Quiller. Report of interview with Bundesminister Ernst Lobst, true name Heinrich Zossen. General picture of imminent operation planned by Phönix organization is as follows."

The mechanism was simple enough and the pivotal factor was that the new German General Staff commanding the Bundeswehr in present-day West Germany had 500,000 fully equipped troops under arms. In West Berlin the British, American, and French troops totaled 12,000. The odds were thus worse than forty to one.

The operation was to be launched in two fast and successive phases: the creation of a cold war crisis by an armed breach of the Berlin Wall and an attack by ground troops on the Allied garrisons in the west of the city. Air bombardment of East Berlin would provoke Russian counteraction at a time when Moscow and all Russian military bases would be suffering the outbreak of pneumonic plague.

The tape spools turned silently.

"Reference Dr. Solomon Rothstein. Please see my report 134A, following decipherment of Rothstein document. Now repeat: Rothstein was doubling with Phönix. His own plan to start an epidemic of pneumonic plague in Argentina was unknown to Phönix. His second and concurrent plan was known to them: he was in fact working for them and under their orders. They asked him to prepare nine capsules of heavily cultured pneumonic plague bacillus for special-messenger transit to Moscow and the eight major Russian military bases. These capsules were to be broken open in those nine centers and the bacillus introduced into foodstuffs four days prior to the air bombardment of East Berlin, so that Russian forces counterreacting in East Germany would be cut off from central directive and military supplies and reinforcements."

This was what I had come to think of as the Parallel Assumption. I knew that Solly Rothstein had been doubling with Phönix. It thus seemed reasonable to assume that he was doing two jobs in parallel: preparing to wipe out San Caterina in Argentina and preparing to wipe out the military centers of whatever country or countries Phönix planned to attack. Solly would never have told me of his Argentina operation. He *had* wanted to tell me of the work he was doing for Phönix. Later, had he lived, he would have informed both Russia and the Allied commands in Berlin, the moment Phönix asked him to produce the nine capsules. The operation would then be imminent and although he might not be given the actual date of its launching he would have five days' warning: one day for transmission of the capsules, four days for the plague to incubate. Certain of this ample period of warning, he passed no information out to the Allied Commands or the Soviets, since his idea was to let Phönix build up their large-scale preparations so that when he sprang the leak they would be caught at the height of their endeavors and would thus serve long sentences.

I said into the tape: "The Rothstein capsules would of course have contained a harmless culture. The instant Phönix knew he was doubling, they shot him and raided his laboratory to seize any papers that might incriminate them. At the same time they would have forced the laboratory assistants to indicate the most lethal of those bacilli then in culture, so that they could proceed with their plan to wipe out the nine Soviet centers, knowing that if Rothstein were doubling he could never have been expected to provide 'live' capsules. Every effort should clearly be made to trace any culture missing from the Rothstein laboratory and to grill both the assistants and the Phönix agents who made the raid. The safe was broken open (see report by Captain Stettner, Z Commission), and it seems probable that an envelope addressed to the Russian Army Command and/or the Allied Commands would have been left there by Dr. Rothstein and subsequently removed and destroyed by Phönix. The raid was carried out in haste, so that the metal container addressed to the doctor's brother was overlooked, whereas almost no *papers* were left behind."

I cut the switch and sat for a minute, checking all mental hooks for material. It seemed about everything.

Pol asked: "Signal ends?"

"I don't know. Probably. There'll be a whole lot of details but there's no time now. Push it through if you want to."

Two of them linked up the tape to the London line for the playback while Pol dialed on the other phone. In a minute he said: "General Stewart, please. Then find out where he is. This is LCB." He watched the men rigging the tape. "General Stewart? Our man is back ahead of schedule. You can go in when you're ready." He hung up.

The tape was running fast, reversed. Hengel spoke into the phone and asked for London. Pol sat on the edge of the desk and looked down at me.

"What happened to Zossen?"

I felt angry with him, and looked directly up at him so that the anger could drive out the other thing they'd all seen in my eyes. Pol was a persnickety man and he remembered everything. He remembered what I'd said to him in the box at the theater when we'd been talking about Zossen. I had said: "Give me a rope, and ask no questions."

"I don't know," I told him.

He said: "I mean do we have to put out smoke for you?"

"No. He left a suicide note. I thought it was the best way."

Pol nodded and moved from the desk as London came on the

line. They started the playback, and as the spools began turning I slid forward on the chair and leaned my head on the wall and closed my eyes. My voice sounded very tired on the tape. I must be getting old, getting old.

LaVergne, TN USA
30 June 2010
187911LV00001B/72/A